BY THE SAME AUTHOR

The Rip and Red Series
illustrated by Tim Probert

A Whole New Ballgame
Rookie of the Year
Tournament of Champions
Most Valuable Players

The Sluggers Series
with Loren Long

Magic in the Outfield
Horsin' Around
Great Balls of Fire
Water, Water Everywhere
Blastin' the Blues
Home of the Brave

Picture Books

Shoeless Joe & Black Betsy (illustrated by C. F. Payne)
The Shot Heard 'Round the World (illustrated by C. F. Payne)
Twenty-One Elephants (illustrated by LeUyen Pham)
The Greatest Game Ever Played (illustrated by Zachary Pullen)

Turkey Bowl (illustrated by C. F. Payne)
The Hallelujah Flight (illustrated by John Holyfield)
The Unforgettable Season (illustrated by S. D. Schindler)
The Soccer Fence (illustrated by Jesse Joshua Watson)
Marvelous Cornelius (illustrated by John Parra)
Derek Jeter Presents Night at the Stadium (illustrated by Tom Booth)
Martina & Chrissie (illustrated by Brett Helquist)

A HIGH FIVE FOR GLENN BURKE

A HIGH FIVE FOR GLENN BURKE

Phil Bildner

Farrar Straus Giroux
New York

Farrar Straus Giroux Books for Young Readers
An imprint of Macmillan Publishing Group, LLC
120 Broadway, New York, NY 10271

Printed in the United States of America by LSC Communications, Harrisonburg,
Virginia
Designed by Cassie Gonzales
First edition, 2020
10 9 8 7 6 5 4 3 2 1

mackids.com

Library of Congress Cataloging-in-Publication Data

Names: Bildner, Phil, author.
Title: A high five for Glenn Burke / Phil Bildner.
Description: First edition. | New York : Farrar Straus Giroux, 2020. |
    Summary: After researching Glenn Burke, the first major league baseball
    player to come out as gay, sixth grader Silas Wade slowly comes out to his
    best friend, Zoey, then his coach, with unexpected consequences.
Identifiers: LCCN 2019009796 | ISBN 9780374312732 (hardcover)
Subjects: | CYAC: Baseball—Fiction. | Schools—Fiction. | Coming
    out—Fiction. | Gays—Fiction. | Best friends—Fiction. |
    Friendship—Fiction. | Family life—Fiction. | Burke, Glenn—Fiction.
Classification: LCC PZ7.B4923 Hig 2020 | DDC [Fic]223
LC record available at https://lccn.loc.gov/2019009796

Our books may be purchased in bulk for promotional, educational, or business use.
Please contact your local bookseller or Macmillan Corporate and Premium Sales
Department at (800) 221-7945 ext. 5442 or by email at
MacmillanSpecialMarkets@macmillan.com.

For Glenn Burke and for every kid who ever questioned or doubted whether they could play sports because of who he, she, or they are. You can play. You belong.

A HIGH FIVE FOR GLENN BURKE

INTRODUCING GLENN BURKE

"Let's do this, Silas," I say to myself.

I'm wearing my baseball uniform in school, and I never wear my baseball uniform here because sixth graders don't wear their baseball uniforms to Hughes Middle School, unless they want to be nonstop teased by the seventh and eighth graders.

But I'm wearing my Renegades uniform today because today's the day. Today's *finally* the day.

I'm standing on my toes and bouncing at the front of Ms. Washington's class. All the tables, chairs, couches, beanbags, gaming rockers, and floor pillows are pushed to the sides. The kids are all off to the sides, too. Some of them are standing, but most are sitting. My best friend, Zoey, is in the back, on one of the green-and-black bungee chairs with her feet up on the armrest of the denim couch.

Ms. Washington let me turn the classroom into a pretend baseball field for my oral presentation on a famous inventor. I used blue painter's tape for the diamond, flattened shoebox tops for the bases, and a balance ball for the pitcher's mound. And projected on the whiteboard behind me is an image of the packed bleachers of Dodger Stadium on a sunny afternoon.

I don't know why I'm so nervous. Actually, I do know why I'm so nervous. I know exactly why I'm so nervous . . .

I take my last breath.

"Introducing Glenn Burke." I pluck the royal-blue Dodgers cap from the stool to my right and slap it on my head. "When Glenn Burke arrived in the big leagues in 1976, the Los Angeles Dodgers thought he was going to be the next Willie Mays. That's like saying a soccer player's going to be the next Messi or a basketball player's going to be the next LeBron."

I grab the yellow Wiffle bat propped against the

stool, flip it up with one hand, and snatch it out of the air with the other. "Glenn Burke was a five-tool talent," I say. "Five-tool talents don't come around that often."

"What's a five-tool talent?" Zoey calls out.

"Good question," I say, pointing the bat.

Zoey learned her lines Wednesday after school. She and I hang out at her house every Wednesday.

"Five-tool talents have all the skills," I say, walking across the room to home plate. "One. Five-tool talents hit for average and put the bat on the ball." I take a swing. "Two. Five-tool talents hit for power and can blast the ball out of any park." I take a bigger swing and watch my imaginary home run soar over the fence. "That ball is outta here!"

I shoot the bat across the floor and jog to first. "Three. Five-tool talents can fly. They steal bases and take extra bases." I run to second, slide, pop up, and then head to third. "Safe!"

I grab my glove off the stool and crow-hop back to the front of the room. "Four," I say. "Five-tool talents can field. They catch everything that comes their way." I pound my glove, feel for the whiteboard, and then pretend I'm taking away a home run with a leaping grab. "Web gem!"

I take the invisible ball out of my glove and fire it back to the infield. "Five. Five-tool talents can throw. Their arms are cannons." I mic-drop my mitt. "Five-tool talents don't come around too often."

I'm killing my oral presentation. Ms. Washington's looking at me the same way she looked at Daphne during her presentation on Lizzie Magie, the woman who invented Monopoly, and the way she looked at Kyle during his presentation on Stephanie Kwolek, the scientist who invented Kevlar, the material used in bulletproof vests. Ms. Washington's big into theater—she always directs the musicals up at the high school—and loves it when kids turn their presentations into performances. That's what Daphne and Kyle did last week, and that's what I'm doing right now.

I peep Zoey, who's double-dimple grinning at me like she does when we're standing on her living room couch singing karaoke. Zoey's got deep dimples in both cheeks, and her double-dimple smile is her super-happy smile.

Zoey knew how badly I wanted to present today. She saw how pumped I was yesterday when Ms. Washington told me I'd be up second this afternoon. But not even

Zoey knows why I didn't want to wait until Monday. Not even Zoey knows why I *needed* to do this today.

"Heading into the final weekend of the 1977 baseball season," I say, "the Los Angeles Dodgers had a chance to make history. No team had ever had four players hit thirty home runs in the same season, but for the Dodgers that year, Steve Garvey, Reggie Smith, and Ron Cey all had more than thirty, and Dusty Baker had twenty-nine." I pick up the Wiffle bat and head back to the plate. "The Los Angeles Dodgers were one Dusty Baker home run away from the record books."

I take a big swing and pretend to miss. Then I take another big swing and pretend to miss again.

"Dusty didn't hit a home run on Friday night," I say. "He didn't hit a home run on Saturday either. He had one last chance on Sunday afternoon, but for the Dodgers to make history, Dusty Baker would have to hit that home run off James Rodney Richard, the hardest-throwing pitcher in all of baseball."

I leave the bat at the plate, head for the balance ball, and pull the old-school Astros lid out of my back pocket. The 'Stros are my favorite team, which is why I have the vintage hat, a Christmas present from last year. I put it on over my Dodgers cap and imitate J. R. Richard's high-kick motion.

"Dusty didn't hit a home run in his first at bat," I say. "He didn't hit a home run in his second at bat either. Dusty had one last chance."

I leave the Astros cap on the balance ball and return to home plate, and as I step back into the pretend batter's box, Zoey starts the music on her phone—the organ music they play at ballgames that gets the fans clapping. Zoey begins to clap, Ms. Washington joins in, and then so do a bunch of other kids.

I brush the number three on the sleeve of my Renegades jersey. I wear number three because Benjamin Franklin Rodriguez, my favorite character from *The Sandlot*—the greatest movie ever made—wore number three when he played for the Dodgers as a grown-up in the movie, which happened to be the number Glenn Burke wore when *he* played for the Dodgers. But I didn't know Glenn Burke wore number three until I was researching him and came across the photo of his 1978 Topps baseball card. When I did, I almost fell off my bed.

"Strike one," I say. "Ball one. Strike two." I stare at the imaginary pitcher and announce the play-by-play.

"One-and-two to Baker. J. R. Richard rocks into his windup, around comes the arm, the one-two pitch . . ."

I take a mighty swing and flip the bat.

"Home run!" I'm still play-by-playing. "Home run!" I raise my arms and start circling the bases. "Dusty Baker has blasted a home run into the bleachers and the Dodgers into the record books. Home run!"

"Dus-ty!" Zoey stands and cheers. "Dus-ty!"

"As Dusty Baker headed for home," I say, slowing down as I round third, "Glenn Burke bolted from the on-deck circle, and as Dusty crossed the plate, Glenn threw his right arm into the air and waved his hand wildly. Dusty smacked Glenn's right hand with his own right hand."

Zoey and I act it out.

"A high five," I say. "The very first high five."

Zoey bows and returns to her seat. I remain at the plate.

"Glenn Burke stepped into the batter's box." I pick up the bat. "Unlike his Dodgers teammates, he hadn't been slugging home runs all season. The rookie was still looking for his very first home run in the big leagues."

I take another mighty swing and flip the bat again.

"Home run!" I say, admiring the make-believe blast. "Home run!" I sprint around the bases and jump on home plate. "When Glenn Burke reached the dugout, his teammates greeted him with handshakes and helmet rubs."

I slap hands with Connor and Kaitlyn and bend down so Nolan and Mia can pat and rub my head.

"Dusty Baker threw his right arm into the air and waved his hand wildly," I say. "And Glenn Burke smacked Dusty's right hand with his own right hand."

Zoey pops back up, and we act it out again.

"A high five," I say. "The second-ever high five. A handshake was born."

I dart back across the diamond, spring off the balance ball, and land in front of the whiteboard.

"Suddenly, the high five was everywhere," I say. I'm up on my toes again and waving my arms. "It spread through baseball. Then it spread through soccer, football, basketball, and hockey. To all sports around the country, to all sports around the world. Soon people were high-fiving in classrooms and courtrooms and boardrooms. On playgrounds and campgrounds and fairgrounds. In movies and on television. Even the pope was high-fiving, and the president of the United States was high-fiving!"

I slide over to Ms. Washington and hold up my hand. She gives me a high five.

Yeah, I'm absolutely killing my oral presentation.

"Nearly a half century later," I say, "the high five lives on and on and on. It's now a universal greeting, known around the globe as a gesture of excitement, a gesture of joy, a gesture of unity, and a gesture we feel in our souls." I thump my chest. "A gesture that began with Glenn Burke, the man who invented the world's most famous handshake."

I let out a breath.

I did it. I actually did it. Nobody knows what I really did, but I did it. I finally did it.

RENEGADES ARE READY

The first pitch to Theo sails outside.

"Hey, pitcher, what's the matter? Why you tryin' to walk our batter?" I chant.

I'm standing on the end of our bench next to Malik, who's my best friend on the Renegades and whose mouthguard's dangling out of his mouth like Steph Curry's. We're leading the cheers in our dugout, and all the other Renegades are lined up next to Malik, and just like we have been all game, we've broken out our rally caps. Whenever we've needed a big hit this afternoon, we've held our caps upside down by the brim and shaken them like rattles at the Titans pitcher. It's worked every time, and in baseball, when something's working, you keep on doing it.

"Let's go, Sixteen." I call Theo by his number. "Be alert, Twenty-One," I shout to Luis on second.

There's one out in the bottom of the last inning, and the game's tied at five, but in my mind, we've already won the game and swept this doubleheader. I know Theo's about to drive Luis in with the winning run because the Titans are playing not to lose, and when you play not to lose against the Renegades, you've already lost.

We schooled them 8–1 in the opener. Theo threw a complete game, striking out nine and giving up only two hits, just like the ace of a staff is supposed to. He was also a beast at the plate, driving in five—three on a home run that landed in the next zip code.

In this game, the Titans led 5–0 after two, and they should've been up by a lot more, and they know it. They left ducks on the pond—runners on base—in the third and fourth, and against the Renegades, you best not waste scoring opportunities, because it's going to come back to haunt you. Inning by inning and run by run, we chipped away, and a minute ago, we tied things up when I scored all the way from first on Luis's base knock to right.

The next pitch lands in the dirt. The catcher blocks the ball with his chest protector, gobbles it up, and checks Luis down at second.

"Hey, pitcher, look at me, I'm a monkey in a tree," I sing.

Malik grabs his mouthguard and starts scratching and making monkey noises. "Ooh-ooh, ee-ee. Ooh-ooh, ee-ee."

"Ooh-ooh, ee-ee!" Ben-Ben, Carter, Jason, and Kareem all join in. "Ooh-ooh, ee-ee!"

I'm always leading the chants, doing whatever I can to keep the Renegades loose and fired up. I'm never able to sit in the dugout, even when I'm not in the game. I'm always hopping on and off the bench, pacing back and forth, rattling the safety fence, and spitting sunflower seeds.

That's what Glenn Burke was like when he played for the Dodgers. Glenn Burke was the life of the dugout. I'm the kid version of Glenn Burke, except I'm not black and built like a tank. I'm white, floppy-haired, and skinny as a rail.

None of my teammates know about my Glenn Burke presentation because I'm the only one on the Renegades who goes to Hughes. I would have never done my project on Glenn Burke if any of the Renegades went to my school.

I still can't believe I did it, but I did. I really did. Now I have to tell Zoey. Yeah, she was in class, but not even she knows what I *really* did. I need to tell her.

I bump Malik with my hip. He bumps me back.

Malik likes to cheer and chant and goof around almost as much as I do. He's not able to sit still either, which is probably why we became friends in the first place. But Malik and I are only baseball-team friends, because we go to different middle schools and live twenty minutes apart. Even though we've been teammates the last three seasons, we've never hung out outside of baseball.

I flip my hair off my face and cup my hand around my mouth. "Hey, pitcher, look at me, I'm a fishy in the sea," I chant.

"Gulp, gulp, guuulp." Malik makes fish noises.

The others join in again. "Gulp, gulp, guuulp!"

The next pitch to Theo is way outside. Ball three. Three balls, no strikes.

"Hey, pitcher, look at me, I'm a kitty in a tree," I sing.

"Meow, meow, meeeow!" Everyone makes cat noises. "Meow, meow, meeeow!"

In the third-base coach's box, Coach Webb holds out his hands and shakes his head. Webb doesn't like it when we taunt the other team, and the only reason he's letting us is that the Titans have been taunting us since the first inning of the opener.

I'm still not used to seeing Webb coaching third. Coach Trent, his brother and the Renegades head coach the last four seasons, has always been our third-base coach, but between games of last week's doubleheader against the Fury, he blew out his Achilles tendon and had to have surgery. He isn't allowed to put any weight on his leg for almost two months, which explains why he's no longer coaching. Malik and I were playing pepper with him when it happened, and we both heard the pop. Ouch!

I miss having Webb in the dugout when we're at bat because he'd always talk baseball and baseball strategy, and I can talk baseball and baseball strategy for hours. Whenever I wasn't on deck or in the hole, I was always next to Webb.

"Renegades are ready," Webb says, swinging his arms and clapping. "Renegades are ready."

"C'mon, Sixteen," I say as Theo adjusts his batting gloves. "A little bingo, a little bingo."

A little bingo is an old-school baseball term that means get a base hit. Even though the count's 3–0 and the Titans pitcher is pitching around Theo, I still know he's getting a hit.

I spit a sunflower seed into the plastic cup stuck in the fence. Pow! I have the best seed-spitting game on the Renegades.

Luis takes his walking lead off second and stares at the pitcher's hand. Luis and I are the fastest kids on the Renegades, and like me, he knows exactly what to do on the basepaths. If the ball's hit on the ground, he takes off; if it's a line drive, he freezes until it clears the infield; and if it's in the air, he laser-locks on Webb at third.

The outfield is playing shallow, because if there's a base hit, it gives them a better chance of throwing Luis out at the plate. But I know Webb doesn't care where the outfielders are playing, because if there's a base hit, he's sending Luis no matter what. Webb's coached only three games at third, and I already know he's a much more aggressive coach than his brother. Make the fielder make the catch, and make the fielder make the throw—that's his approach to the game. Mine too.

Theo taps the plate with his bat and gets into his stance. The Titans pitcher checks Luis and fires the pitch. It's outside again, but not as far outside as the last pitch. Theo reaches across the plate and shoots a line drive into right.

"Yeah, yeah, yeah!" I toss my cap and leap onto the fence. "Yeah, yeah, yeah!"

"Go, go!" Webb shouts as he windmills his arm and gallops down the third-base line. "Go, go!"

Luis had to wait to see if the line drive cleared the infield, but as soon as it did, he took off. He makes the turn at third and heads for the plate. The right fielder fields the ball and throws home, but the ball never makes it, and Luis scores easily.

"Ballgame!" I leap off the fence and race to home plate. "Pow, pow, pow!" I flying-chest-bump Luis and then bolt toward first base. "Pow, pow, pow!" I jumping-chest-bump Theo.

On the infield grass, all the Renegades are elbow-bashing, bro-hugging, and chest-bumping.

"Ballgame!" I double-high-five Malik. We clasp our hands and touch foreheads. "Ballgame!"

3

THE WADE FAMILY

I'm standing on my bed with my laptop resting on my hand when my bedroom door starts to open, and even before I see Mom's face, I slam the laptop shut.

"Silas, please tell me you weren't someplace you weren't supposed to be," she says.

"Oh, hi, Mom." I give her a look that says I wasn't doing anything wrong. It's also a look that says I really wish she wouldn't ask me that every time I close my laptop when she's around. "Nice to see you, too," I say. "Glad you're home."

"Hello, Silas," she says.

I kick out my legs and drop to my bed. Then I bounce backward until I'm leaning against the wall behind my pillows and facing Mom in the doorway.

"And how was your day, Mom?" I ask, still giving her a look.

"It was a Monday," she says, waving her phone.

Ever since Mom left her job last year to open the Jump & Grind, the coffee shop and performance space she's always wanted, her phone's been permanently attached to her hand. She's always reading or sending a text, talking to someone, leaving a voice memo, or adding another to-do item to a to-do list on the to-do app she never closes.

"Silas, do we need to talk about your internet usage?" she asks.

"I don't know, do we?" I hold out the laptop. "Would you like to check my history?"

"Your best friend builds robots and programs computers," she says. "You know all about private browsers, going incognito, deleting your history, and doing whatever you need to do to hide where you've been the instant your father or I appear."

21

"I was on YouTube," I say.

"I'm still scarred by that zit-popping video you and your sister made me watch over the weekend," she says, shaking her head and smiling.

I smile, too. "Yeah, that was pretty nasty, especially when the guy—"

"Stop," she says. "I don't need to relive it."

With her free hand, she presses the pushpins holding my Renegades schedule to the bulletin board hanging next to my door and then runs her fingers over the baseball stickers my younger sister Haley has stuck to the frame. Then she starts straightening the Houston Astros bobbleheads on the shelf above my dresser. They're already perfectly straight because she straightened them last night—and the night before and the night before—when she came in to say good night.

"This looks nothing like José Altuve," Mom says, tapping the bobblehead on the end. She points to the next one. "And this looks nothing like Carlos Correa."

"And that looks nothing like George Springer," I say, nodding to the next one. "And that looks nothing like Alex Bregman. You say the same thing every time you're in my room."

"Not every," she says. "Grace is taking you to practice tomorrow?" It's more a statement than question.

"Yes," I say. Grace is Zoey's older sister.

"Be ready when she comes for you. And be sure to tell her thank you for me."

I strum my laptop. "Always am, always do."

Dad used to take me to baseball practice on Tuesday and Thursday afternoons, but his new boss won't let him leave the office. Dad really wants to quit his job and find a new accounting firm or maybe even start his own—he's a CPA—but he can't because we get our health insurance through his work.

"I don't think I'm going to see you at all tomorrow," Mom says, checking her phone. "I'm opening in the morning, and then by the time you get home from baseball tomorrow night, I'm going to be dead to the world."

I flip the hair off my face. "Sounds like a Tuesday to me."

"Sounds like any day that ends in *day* to me."

When Mom opened the Jump & Grind, her plan was to hire someone to run it for her, but she hasn't been able to find anyone reliable, so she's been working twelve-hour days, six and seven days a week since last August.

Tuesdays are the worst, because in the afternoon, she has to get Haley to gymnastics and my other younger sister, Semaj, to physical therapy. Then she has to get back to the Jump & Grind to close and set up for tomorrow.

"I do like this new woman I hired," Mom says.

"I've heard that one before," I say.

"I think this one's different. She's showing more initiative than the others. A lot more initiative."

I retie the drawstrings on my navy sweats. "We'll see."

"That we will. You're still going to Zoey's on Wednesday?"

"When do I not go to Zoey's on Wednesdays?"

"I'm just checking, Silas. The last thing I want is to show up at her house after working all day and find you're not there."

"When have I not been there?"

She walks over to my bed. "I need to go check on your father and sisters," she says. "Do you need me to come back to tuck you in?"

"I'm okay." I strum my laptop again.

She untwists the strap of my gray tank top undershirt and kisses the top of my head. Her hair smells like

24

coffee. It always does. *She* always does. Mom's like a human coffee-scented air freshener these days.

"Please don't stay up too late." She motions to my laptop.

"I won't."

She starts for the door and stops. "Oh, Silas, we still haven't talked about your project. I can't believe I forgot."

"It's okay," I say again.

"No, it's not okay." She smacks her phone against her leg. "It's really not."

"Sounds like someone needs a self-care day."

"You got that right," she says. "I really . . . I can't keep going like this."

"Then take a self-care day."

"If only it were that easy."

Mom's big on self-care, and she's always saying that when you take better care of yourself, you're more productive, less stressed, and better at decision-making. But lately, she hasn't exactly been taking her own advice.

"You gave that presentation three days ago, Silas," she says. "I want to hear about it. I really do. Let me finish getting everything organized for tomorrow, and as soon as I—"

"Monster!" Semaj runs into my room. She's dripping wet and completely naked. "Monster!" she shouts. "Monster!"

I cover my laptop with my pillow because out-of-control and soaking wet four-year-olds don't get near my Chromebook.

"I'm going to get you!" Dad jumps into the doorway and flicks the light switch.

"Must you, Gil?" Mom makes a face.

"I'm going to get you!" he says, ignoring Mom. He shakes the *Moana* bath towel like a matador and charges in. "I'm going to—"

Semaj screams, a painful, high-pitched, top-of-her-lungs screech. My hands shoot to my ears.

"Semaj!" Mom shouts. "No!"

Semaj keeps screeching.

"Semaj!" Dad yells. He wraps her in the bath towel and holds her against his body. "Semaj! Semaj!"

Finally, she stops.

Semaj is a screamer. The first time it happened was over Christmas break at the Olive Garden, which was the last time we ate at a restaurant as a family. Then it happened at Kroger, and then it happened outside the

Jump & Grind, and when it did, Mom cried. It won't happen at baseball, because I've made them both promise not to bring her.

Semaj is James spelled backward. (It's pronounced SE as in *second* and MAJ as in *majesty*.) Semaj was supposed to be a boy—at least according to every sonogram—and my parents were going to name her James. But a few weeks before delivery, they found out she was going to be a girl, which was the same time they found out she was a breech baby, coming out feet first instead of headfirst. Since everything about the new baby was backward and unexpected, my parents decided to reverse the name they'd chosen.

"Why do you encourage her like that, Gil?" Mom glares.

"I wasn't encouraging her, Erica," he snaps.

"You weren't exactly helping."

"I wasn't exactly helping?" He's still holding Semaj and trying to dry her off. "What do you think I've been doing since I got home?"

"That's not what I meant," Mom says.

"She's taken all her meds, her teeth are brushed, and I've given her the bath you ordered me to give her the second I walked in." He shakes his head. "Cut me a break, Erica."

Mom turns and dips her head into the hall. "Enough with the cartwheels, Haley!" she shouts. "I don't want to spend the night at urgent care."

Whenever my parents argue, Haley always starts doing backflips, handsprings, and cartwheels because she knows how much they hate it when she does gymnastics in the house and she thinks it will distract them.

"How's it going, Swade?" Dad finally greets me.

"Fine."

"How was school?"

"Good."

Swade is a combination of my first and last name, Silas Wade. Dad's the only one who still calls me it, and I really wish he wouldn't, but I know how much it means to him because he's the one who gave me the nickname when I was little. Mom knows I can't stand that he still calls me Swade, but she won't say anything because she says it's my place to tell him, not hers.

"How'd that presentation of yours go today?" Dad asks, his arms still wrapped tightly around Semaj. "The one about the guy who invented the high five."

"It was Friday," I say.

"Friday? Oh, I thought it was . . . So how did it go?"

Haley walks in before I can answer. She's holding Semaj's polka-dotted onesie pajamas and *Croc and Ally*, the book she reads to Semaj every night at bedtime. She hands the pajamas to Dad and then does a split on the floor by my workstation.

"Look at us," Dad says as he puts the onesie on Semaj. "The five of us together in one room. Who says we never spend quality time together anymore?"

"Quality?" I say.

"Well, no one's yelling at the moment, right?" Dad smiles. He pats Semaj on her behind and taps Haley's with his foot. "Let's go, girls. Story time."

Haley springs to her feet and races out of my room.

"G'night, Swade." Dad picks up Semaj and holds out his hand for a high five.

I tap it softly.

"How are Semaj's meds?" Mom looks up from her phone as Dad heads for the door. "Does she need any refills?"

"Blue pills, blue pills," Semaj answers.

Mom kisses Semaj on the top of her head and smiles. "The blue pills?"

"Blue pills, blue pills," Semaj says again, and taps Mom's head. "Beep, beep."

"Beep, beep." Mom half smiles and taps Semaj's head.

"I'll check to see how many are left after they're in bed," Dad says. "If I need to stop off before picking Swade up at practice tomorrow, I will."

"Please don't forget," she says.

"I won't forget." He walks out.

I can't remember the last time I heard my parents have a conversation about something other than needing to pick something up, needing to pick someone up, Haley's gymnastics, Semaj's medication, my baseball, insurance companies, Dad's boss, or the Jump & Grind.

"You won't stay up too late?" Mom says to me.

"I won't."

"I love you, Silas."

As soon as the door closes behind her, I flip the hair off my face and open my laptop.

ZOEY AND GRACE

"You look hilarious, Silas," Zoey says from the front seat.

"So rad." Grace glances at me in the rearview. "Man, I wish we could stick around to watch this."

I shake my cleats off my hands and strum the front console with my sock-covered fingers. "This is going to be nuts," I say.

Grace is driving me to baseball practice, but I'm not wearing my usual practice jersey and sweats. I'm wearing my Renegades uniform, but I have it on inside out, backward, and upside down—and by upside down, I mean I'm wearing my pants over my head and arms and my jersey on my legs.

"You sure you can't stay for a few minutes?" I say, bouncing in the middle of the back seat of the Kia.

"Nah, man," Grace says as she accelerates through a yellow light. "Gotta get to work."

"The Playhouse isn't work," I say.

"Yo, I do love my job, but it is work."

Grace works at the local theater. She's in charge of the sets and costumes for the shows, and in a few weeks, they're putting on *Bye Bye Birdie*. My teacher Ms. Washington's actually the one who got Grace interested in theater in the first place. When Grace went to Hughes, she had Ms. Washington for ELA, too, and in high school, Grace was the stage manager of all the shows Ms. Washington directed.

"I'd stay to watch," Zoey says, "but I need to get to the rec center for robotics."

"I know, I know," I say. "Three weeks till the big tourney."

"The same weekend as *Bye Bye Birdie*," Zoey says.

Later in the month, Zoey's robotics club is competing in this all-county middle school tournament. Even though she's only in sixth grade and all the other kids are in seventh and eighth, Zoey's the best one on her team.

"I'm not going to wear this," I say, stuffing the Ghostface mask into my baseball bag. "I can't get it to stay."

"You don't need it," Zoey says. "I'm telling you, you look hilarious without it."

I take out my phone and peep myself in my camera. I really do look hilarious. My pants are on backward over my head and pulled down to below my shoulders so that the belt is around my chest. My head is up one of the pant legs so you can see the outline of my face in the fabric, and I'm able to see because I made tiny slits where my eyes are. I'm wearing my jersey backward over my legs so that my number three is upside down over my crotch, and the word RENEGADES is upside down over my butt. I wanted the Ghostface mask in the neck hole below my crotch, but no matter how far I stuffed it in, it kept falling out. And under my jersey, I have on a long-sleeve shirt that reaches all the way to my bare feet.

"Glenn Burke always used to do stuff like this when he was on the Dodgers," I say.

"Who's Glenn Burke?" Grace asks as we stop at a light.

"The guy who invented the high five," Zoey answers.

Grace glances at me in the rearview again. "Someone invented the high five?"

"Glenn Burke," I say.

"Silas did his presentation on him," Zoey says. "He turned it into this whole performance. Ms. Washington ate it up."

"I bet she did," Grace says.

"Glenn Burke was an outfielder for the Dodgers in the 1970s," Zoey says. "A five-tool talent."

"Just like me," I say. I hoist myself up and motion with my sock-covered hands to the number over my crotch. "And he wore number three just like me."

"Dopeness," Grace says.

"But I don't wear number three because of Glenn Burke," I say. "I wear number three because Benjamin Franklin Rodriguez wore number three when he played for the Dodgers in *The Sandlot*."

"Which, according to Silas Wade," Zoey says, double-dimple grinning, "is the greatest film ever made."

"Pow!" I say. "Did you know there's a huge mistake in *The Sandlot*? In the opening scene, after Benny gets out of the pickle, Ham and Bertram—"

"The pickle?" Grace says.

"A rundown," I say. "He gets in a pickle between third and home, and after he gets out of it, Ham and Bertram, and I'm pretty sure Smalls, give Benny high fives. So does either Timmy or Tommy Timmons—it's hard to tell." I strum the front console again. "Hello! That would've been impossible in 1962 because the high five wasn't invented until 1977."

"Right on," Grace says, changing lanes. "I love finding anachronisms in movies and shows."

"Anach-cro-say-what?" I ask.

"Anachronisms," she says. "Chronological errors. Like in the movie *Back to the Future*, in the scene where Marty McFly plays 'Johnny B. Goode,' the Gibson guitar he's playing didn't exist in 1955. Anachronisms."

"Glenn Burke loved doing imitations," I say, laughing. "This one time, he stuffed pillows under his jersey and waddled around the dugout like Tommy Lasorda, the Dodgers manager."

"So he liked to goof around, he liked to imitate people, and he liked being the center of attention," Grace says. "Yo, I'm beginning to understand this connection."

"You don't know the half of it," I say.

"What do you mean?" Zoey asks.

"Nothing, nothing," I say quickly.

I don't know why I said that. Then again, I *do* know why I said it.

"Um, thanks for taking me today," I say to Grace as she turns in to Field of Dreams, the sports complex where we have all our practices and games.

"Yo, you never have to thank me for driving you," Grace says. "You know that."

"Erica says I do," I say.

"She knows you don't either."

"Dolores appreciates that you say thank you," Zoey says. Dolores is Grace and Zoey's mom. "She knows you always—"

"Is she shooting any parties this week?" I ask.

"Every weekend from now till the end of June," Grace answers. "Wedding season has begun."

Dolores is a photographer. She shoots all kinds of parties and events—weddings, bar mitzvahs, quinceañeras, graduations, anniversaries, sweet sixteens. She also has her own studio.

"Instead of letting me out in the usual spot," I say as Grace pulls into the drop-off circle, "can you leave me

36

over there by the batting cages?" I motion with my socked hand. "I don't want anyone to see me yet."

"Right on," Grace says.

"You need help getting out?" Zoey asks as we pull up to the curb.

"I think I'm good." I grab my cleats off the floor, loop my arm through my bag, and open the door. Then I slide out and hip-check the door closed. "This is going to be nuts!"

Zoey lowers the front window. "You really do look hilarious," she says.

"We want vids, man," Grace says, leaning across the front seat.

I clap my cleats and then raise my arms and sway from side to side like I would at a concert.

They both laugh.

"See you tomorrow, Zoey," I say. "Go kick some bot butt."

She knocks the car door and double-dimple grins. "Go kick some goofball, baseball butt."

EPIC!

I'm over by the batting cages watching my teammates get ready for practice. Ben-Ben, Jason, and Luis are sitting on the grass along the first-base line, while the rest of the Renegades, including Webb and Coach Rockford, are behind the backstop. The only ones who aren't here yet are Malik, Brayden, and Brayden's dad—Coach Noles—who became an assistant coach when Coach Trent went down.

I pull the sleeves of my shirt down over my ankles and take a breath because right now, I'm still thinking about what I said to Zoey or, rather, what I *almost* said to Zoey.

I'm telling her tomorrow. That means, tomorrow's the day. Tomorrow's the day everything changes, and I do mean *everything*.

I spot Brayden's dad's car pulling into a spot and start walking around the far side of the batting cages until I reach the end of the fence down the left-field line. Then I wait for all the Renegades to be by the backstop.

"Let's do this, Silas," I say when they finally are.

I take off running toward the infield with my arms straight up over my head and my cleats pointed toward the sky. I'm moving my arms back and forth the way I'd kick my legs if I were swimming because I loved how funny this looked when I practiced it in the mirror in Mom and Dad's closet.

Ben-Ben spots me first as I'm approaching third base.

"Dude!" He points. "Dude!"

"Check out Silas!" Luis shouts. "No way!"

I rotate my wrists so that my cleats move in all different directions and sway my arms like I did for Zoey and Grace when I got out of the car.

"Ha!" Jason shouts. "Silas!"

"Epic!" Malik raises his arms.

I spin around and wiggle my butt.

"You're such a weirdo, Silas!" Theo says, laughing.

"I know, right?" Kareem says. "Such a weirdo."

All the Renegades—including the three coaches—are now standing and looking my way, and everyone is smiling or laughing.

Halfway down the third-base line, I stop and stand on one foot. I hold out my arms like I'm trying to keep my balance and rock in all directions because this move looked hilarious in my parents' mirror, too.

"You da man, Silas!" Webb shouts.

I bounce-walk the rest of the way down the third-base line, and as I do, Luis and Ben-Ben are laughing so hard they're literally rolling around on the grass. Before I reach the plate, I stop and slowly bend forward until my cleats almost touch my toes. Then I stand back up, lean left, right, backward, and then wobble and stumble across home.

"Epic!" Malik races up and puts his baseball cap over my head, which is still in my pant leg.

I start hopping on one leg, but as soon as I do, the

cap falls off. When I try picking it up with my cleats, I can't grip it. Then Webb gives me a gentle push, and when he does, I pretend he shoved me hard, fling the cap into the air, and fall over. Then I roll onto my back, raise my arms and legs, and shake them.

Everyone's laughing. I love hearing all the Renegades laughing.

WEBB IN CHARGE

I put my uniform on the correct way for the team stretch, which is how we start every practice. Malik's my partner, and right now we're working our hamstrings, the last muscles we stretch before running and conditioning. For hamstring stretches, one person lies on the grass on his back with his leg straight up, while the other person leans in and slowly presses the leg a little higher. All the Renegades take stretching seriously, even though we like to goof around, talk, and eat.

I'm lying on the grass on my back, and Malik's

pressing against my heel. With his free hand, he's eating a blueberry muffin, and he's eating it the way he always eats his muffins, first the stump, then the top. I can tell the muffin he's holding is loaded with blueberries because they're glistening in the sun, just like Malik's eyes.

"Dude, what are you staring at?" he asks.

"Huh?"

"What are you staring at?"

But before I can answer, he shakes his head so that some of the crumbs fly out and land on me.

"Nasty!" I say, swatting them away.

"I'm sharing my muffin with you." Malik laughs, and more crumbs shoot from his mouth. "Never again can you accuse me of hogging my muffin tops."

"Switch it up, Renegades," Brayden says.

At every practice, a different player leads the stretches, and today it's Brayden's turn.

I hold out my hand so Malik can pull me up, but when he takes it, I grab his arm with my other hand and pull him to the ground and jump to my feet. I then brush the crumbs still on the front of my jersey onto him.

"You can never accuse me of hogging my muffin tops," I say.

He swats them off.

"How'd you come up with that upside-down uniform idea?" Malik asks, rolling onto his back and raising his right leg.

"How do you think?"

"YouTube," he says.

Malik knows I spend most of my non-baseball-playing, non-sleeping, and non-going-to-school hours on YouTube.

I rest his ankle on my shoulder, lean forward, and slowly push his leg toward him. "I found this video of a New York Mets player from the 1980s dressed like that," I say. "Everyone thought it was the funniest thing ever—the players, the announcers, even the other team."

I found the video accidentally, which is how I find most things on YouTube. A video ends, the next one autoplays, and I end up watching it. That's what happened with this. I was watching baseball-blooper videos, and after one, the video of the Mets player started.

That's how I discovered Glenn Burke last year. I was watching highlights of the 2017 World Series—when my Astros beat the Los Angeles Dodgers—and after one video, a video about the Astros–Dodgers rivalry from the

1970s to the 1990s started. Back then, they were in the same division in the National League. Then a video about the Los Angeles Dodgers teams from the 1970s began to play, and then a video about Glenn Burke came on.

"Other leg, Renegades," Brayden calls out.

I jump back so Malik can drop his right leg and raise his left, but before I put his ankle on my shoulder, I grab his sunglasses out of his glove and put them on over my cap.

"Who am I?" I ask. I pretend I'm trying to catch a pop-up and shield my eyes from the sun with my hand. "I got it! I got it." I then watch the make-believe ball fall to the ground. "I don't got it."

Ben-Ben and Luis are stretching beside us. They both bust out laughing.

"Dude, I've never lost a ball in the sun during a game," Malik says.

"It's only a matter of time," I say.

Malik holds up a fist. "Never!"

"Webb's going to go nuts the first time you do," I say.

"Never going to happen."

During games, Malik sometimes wears his sunglasses on top of his cap because he likes the way it looks.

Ben-Ben, Luis, and some of the other Renegades do the same thing. The coaches can't stand it. They say if you're going to wear sunglasses, wear them on your eyes or don't wear them at all. I know it's only a matter of time before someone loses a ball in the sun while their sunglasses are on top of their cap, and when that happens, I want to be in a galaxy far, far away.

"How funny would it be if it happens when your mom is ringing her cowbell?" I say, laughing.

"Never going to happen," he says again.

Malik's mom sometimes brings a cowbell to our games, and he hates that she does. Whenever she rings it, he covers his face with his glove. It can get pretty annoying, and one time last year, a bunch of parents from the other team asked her not to ring it as much . . . And none of the parents from our team stood up for her.

"Okay, gentlemen," Webb says, waving us over. "Let's bring it in."

We bring it in by the safety fence in front of the first-base dugout. I sway from foot to foot because I'm never able to stand still during these minimeetings.

"We have two big games this weekend against the Thunder," Webb says.

"After which the Renegades will be seven and one," Theo says.

"Yeah." Kareem holds out his fist to Theo, but Theo leaves him hanging. "After which . . . after which we'll be seven and one."

"We go one game at a time," Webb says. He blows into his hands and then tucks them into the pouch of his blue Renegades hoodie. "Let's not get ahead of ourselves."

Theo and Kareem are right. We should be 7–1 after this weekend, but we really should be 8–0. The only game we lost was against the Fury right after Coach Trent got hurt. If we do sweep the Thunder this weekend, we'll be in first place with a two-game lead in the standings. Even if we go only .500 the rest of the way, we still make the playoffs . . . But the Renegades are not going only .500 the rest of the way.

"We do go one game at a time," Coach Noles says, "but heading into the bye week on a hot streak isn't a bad thing."

"Hear, hear," Coach Rockford adds.

We don't have games next weekend because of Easter, but we still have practices on Tuesday and Thursday.

"A few housekeeping items before we start our

station work," Webb says. "As you know, I'm trying not to change things too much from the way Coach Trent ran the show. But I am making a few tweaks here and there, and I'm making one of those tweaks right now."

"Uh-oh," Theo says, smiling.

"Yeah, uh-oh." Webb nods and smiles back. "Coach Trent let you text him if you couldn't make a practice or game. No more. If you can't make a practice or game, I want to hear from you. Not your mom, not your dad, from you. I get a phone call, not a text."

"Why the change?" Coach Noles asks.

Webb looks at Coach Noles. "Because that's the way I want things done," he says.

"No reason?" Coach Noles says.

I'm swaying from foot to foot a little faster. It's weird when Coach Noles and Webb go back and forth like this. It's not the first time they have, and I'm not the only one who's noticed. Ben-Ben, Luis, and Malik have all said something about it, too.

"If you can't make it to a practice or game," Webb says, "I want to hear it from you."

"I don't see how it makes much of a difference," Coach Noles says.

"Then it shouldn't matter."

Coach Noles folds his arms. "Does this new rule apply to coaches' kids? And coaches' nephews?"

Webb pauses. "It most certainly does," he says. "Rules apply to everyone. Full stop."

"Hear, hear." Coach Rockford gives a thumbs-up. "Renegades are responsible."

When Coach Trent got hurt, it was never a thing that Webb became the head coach and Coach Rockford stayed assistant coach, because Coach Rockford didn't want to be head coach. But when Coach Noles became an assistant, I'm pretty sure he thought he'd have more say. When he was a parent in the bleachers, he was always shouting at Coach Trent to bring in Brayden to pitch and to make changes, but Coach Trent rarely listened, and Webb rarely listens now.

"We're taking five laps around the field today, gentlemen," Webb says.

"Five?" a few kids say at the same time.

"You heard me," Webb says, pulling his hand out of his pouch and holding it up. "It will help keep you warm out here. Five sprints."

That was another one of Webb's tweaks. At the start

of practice, Coach Trent always had us jog a lap or two around the field, but Webb makes us sprint.

"I for one want to see you pushing yourselves out there," Webb says. "Go hard. And then when you finish, check in with Coach Noles."

Coach Noles waves his clipboard. "I have your individual assignments," he says.

"We have four stations this afternoon," Webb says. "Hitting—"

"Hitting, agility and speed, infield, and outfield," Coach Noles interrupts.

Webb pauses again. "Hitting, agility and speed, infield, and outfield," he says. "As you go from station to station, we've targeted specific skill areas we want you focusing on. Put in the extra work this afternoon."

"Hear, hear," Coach Rockford says.

"Now I've got one more tweak." Webb holds up a finger.

"You just said it was only one tweak right now," Ben-Ben says, smiling.

"One tweak then, one tweak now," Webb says. "Renegades, take a knee."

He waits for everyone to kneel.

"Everyone here knows how I feel about the taunting," he says. "I'd prefer you didn't, but if you're getting it from the other team, I'm not going to stop you. But I am putting a stop to the monkey taunts. No more monkey-in-a-tree chants, no more monkey sounds, and no more monkey scratching."

"Why not?" Theo asks.

"Because people might think you're being racist," Webb answers.

"We're not being racist," I say.

"We know you're not." Webb motions to Coach Rockford and Coach Noles. "But someone else might think that you are."

"How's it being racist?" Theo asks.

"Making monkey gestures and making monkey sounds is racist," Coach Rockford answers.

"How?" Kareem asks.

"When fans taunt black athletes with monkey chants, those fans are being racist," Coach Rockford says. "When soccer fans do it, the clubs get penalized."

"But that's not why we're doing it," I say.

"We know you're not," Webb says again. "On the Renegades, we have black kids, brown kids—"

"A black coach," Coach Rockford interrupts.

"A black coach," Webb says, motioning to Coach Rockford. "We have kids from all over. But all it takes is one person." He holds up a finger again. "If one person thinks we're being racist, we're being racist."

"Hear, hear," Coach Rockford says. "Perception is reality."

"That's exactly it," Webb says. "If one person decides that it is an issue, it becomes an issue. So in order to avoid having it become an issue, we're not doing it anymore. Full stop."

I stand as soon as Webb says "full stop" because I can only take a knee for so long.

"Wait," I say, shaking out my legs and smiling. "There's one more thing."

Malik starts to crack up because that's how well he knows me, and he already realizes what I'm about to do. I'm about to imitate Webb. I used to imitate Coach Trent all the time—the way he kicked at the dirt when someone made a mental error, the way he chewed his gum, and the way he stood in the dugout with his arms folded and hand on his chin—but this will be the first time I'm imitating Webb in front of everyone.

"We're taking five laps around the field today, gentlemen," I say in a deep voice. "Five sprints. Push yourselves. Go hard."

Everyone's laughing.

"I for one want to see you putting in the extra work this afternoon." I swing my arms and clap like Webb when he's coaching third. "Renegades are ready. Renegades are ready!"

Webb smiles and pumps his fist at me.

I needed to lighten things up and get us back into a baseball-playing frame of mind. That's what Glenn Burke would have done.

7

GLENN BURKE WAS...

I'm sitting cross-legged on the floor of my bedroom, leaning against the side of my workstation. I check my door again to make sure the light in the hallway is still out.

Everyone's asleep and has been for a while. Mom was already asleep when Dad and I got home from practice, like she said she'd be, which is why my dirty baseball clothes are still on the floor and I didn't get yelled at for it. Semaj was also asleep. I was glad she was, and so was Dad, but he would never admit it. Only Haley was awake. She did splits on the kitchen floor while Dad and I ate the chicken-salad sandwiches and muffins Mom had brought home for us from the Jump & Grind. Dad did let Haley have a piece of his muffin even though she'd already brushed her teeth, but only after she pinky swore not to say anything to Mom.

I stare at the laptop that's sitting on my knees. I'm reading the same article I've read over and over and over these last few weeks, the one about Glenn Burke from way back in 1982 that ran in a magazine called *Inside Sports*.

There's so much more to Glenn's story than what I shared in class. I didn't share the part about his secret, the secret he kept from his family, his friends, and his teammates. And I didn't share the part about when his secret began to get out and the whispers around him grew louder and louder and louder, how Al Campanis, the vice president of the Los Angeles Dodgers, called Glenn into his office.

Glenn wasn't married, and most of the other players on the team were. Back then, the Dodgers wanted their players to be married. It fit their image—clean-cut, family-friendly, and all-American. So Al Campanis offered Glenn thousands of dollars to find a girlfriend and get married.

"Al, I don't think I'll be getting married no time soon," Glenn told him.

Glenn Burke was gay. That was his secret. That was the secret the Dodgers knew and didn't want anyone to find out. It didn't matter that he was their five-tool talent who was supposed to be the next Willie Mays. And it didn't matter that he was their starting center fielder for the opening game of the World Series against the New York Yankees at Yankee Stadium.

The Dodgers *couldn't* have a gay player on their team. The Dodgers *couldn't* have a gay person in their organization.

I flip the hair off my face and wipe my eyes with my palms. That's the part I didn't share about Glenn Burke, the biggest part of all.

8

OUT

"I need to tell you something," I say to Zoey.

"Never heard of that song," she says. "Who sings it?"

We're in Zoey's living room singing karaoke like we always do Wednesday after school. We're here by ourselves—her mom's at work, and Grace is at the Playhouse.

"Can you sit for a sec?" I say.

Zoey's standing on the gray sectional sofa. I'm sitting on the floor next to the glass coffee table.

"What are we singing next?" She points her mic at

the song titles on the wall-mounted flat screen. "Some old-school Eminem? 'Lose Yourself'?"

"Can you sit?"

"'Hakuna Matata'!" She waves her mic like a wand. "It means no worries for the rest of your days."

"I know what it means," I say.

I'm not thinking about what we're singing next. All I'm thinking about is what I promised myself I'd tell Zoey as soon as we set foot inside her house. But I didn't, so now all I'm thinking about is what I promised myself I'd tell her as soon as we finished singing "Can't Stop the Feeling!" But I didn't, so now all I'm thinking about is what I promised myself I'd tell her as soon as we finished singing "All Night Long."

I put my mic on the sofa cushion and wipe my drenched forehead with my forearm. "Sit for a sec," I say.

"This really can't wait?"

My look tells her it can't.

"Grrrr," she says. "This had better be good, Silas." She plops down, crosses her legs, and puts her mic next to mine. "What?"

I stare at the two pretend mics Zoey made for us a few weeks ago using tennis balls, gauze, silver spray paint, paper towel tubes, old phone chargers, and duct tape.

"You're just going to sit here and not say anything?" she says.

I can feel my heart beating against the inside of my chest. This isn't going as planned. This is going the opposite of planned. I can't get myself to say the words. I've rehearsed this conversation thousands of times—lying in bed, in the shower, standing out in center field, talking to my stuffed animals, in the mirror in my parents' closet, before the—

"Fine, I'll talk," Zoey says. "I'm missing so much school these next few weeks because of the robotics tournament, and I've started telling my teachers, and the only one who's been halfway cool about it is Ms. Washington. Everyone else is being so annoying. They're saying I'm going to have to make up the work and—" She picks up her mic and twirls it. "Why are you sweating like you just—"

"Glenn Burke was gay," I say.

She points the mic. "That's what you had to tell me?"

"He was . . . he was the first major league baseball player to come out as gay."

"We stopped karaoke so you could tell me Glenn Burke was gay? This is what couldn't wait?"

"He didn't officially come out until after he stopped playing—"

"Officially?" Zoey cuts me off and laughs. "Is that when he got his membership card?"

"You know what I mean," I say. I'm not laughing. I run my fingertip along the parquet wood floor. "People knew he was gay, but he didn't openly admit it until he retired."

"Glenn Burke was gay." Zoey twirls her mic again. "Great. Now can we get back to—"

"I think I might be gay."

Zoey stares but doesn't say anything.

I stare back and wait, wait for her to say something, wait for her to say anything.

"Oh," she says.

I swallow and nod.

"Like . . . like Glenn Burke," she says. "Really?"

I nod again.

"Are you sure?"

"Kinda . . . I mean, yeah. Yeah, yes."

"Okay."

She smiles, but it's not a real Zoey smile, because I know Zoey's smiles. I wait for her to say something more, anything more.

"Okay," she says again. "Cool."

"Yeah?" My voice shakes.

She smiles again, and it's still not a real Zoey smile, but it's closer.

I breathe. "Thanks."

"So that's why you did your report on him?"

"I had to."

"But you didn't say anything about his being gay."

"But I did my report on him. I did my report on a . . ." I close my eyes and cover my face with my hands.

"What?" Zoey touches my leg. "What is it?"

I shake my head but don't answer.

"Tell me," she says. "What?"

I keep shaking my head.

"Silas, you know—"

Suddenly, I reach for Zoey and hug her, and she hugs me back, and if ever there was a moment when I needed a hug, it is this moment right now. I start to cry, harder than I've cried in the longest time and harder than I've ever cried in front of Zoey. She keeps hugging me and doesn't let go until I finally do.

"Wow," I say, wiping my eyes with my palms again. "That's the first time . . . that's the first time I've ever said it out loud . . . to anyone."

Zoey's double-dimple grinning, and if ever there was a moment I needed Zoey to be double-dimple grinning, it is this moment right now.

"I'm still shaking." I hold out my trembling hands.

"I see that."

"You have no idea . . ." I don't finish the sentence. Zoey's double-dimple smile is no longer a double-dimple smile. It's a not real Zoey smile again. "What?"

"Nothing," she says.

"What?"

She picks up her mic and touches my cheek.

I push it away.

She touches my other cheek with it.

"No," I say. "Stop."

"Why were you so worried to tell me?"

"I just was." I flip the hair off my face.

"There he is." Zoey points the mic. "There's the floppy-haired Silas Wade we know and love."

"Thanks," I say.

"You knew I'd be fine with it," she says. "How could you think I wouldn't be?"

"I don't know . . . I . . . this is just between us. Okay, Zoey?"

"Okay."

"I mean it. No one else."

"Of course. I know."

"Promise, Zoey?"

"Promise, Silas." She taps my leg with the mic. "I need some ice cream."

9

CALLING, NOT TEXTING

My phone buzzes.

Zoey: **Hey!**

Zoey: **Just got home.**

Me: **hey. give me a sec.**

"I'm out," I say to Haley. I drop *Croc and Ally* onto the pad of stickers in her lap and slide off Semaj's bed. "I need to talk to Zoey."

"You mean your girlfriend?" Haley giggles.

"Zo, Zo." Semaj laughs.

I ignore them.

I didn't think Zoey was going to text me back, even though Zoey always texts me back. I knew that she had robotics until late and that she was probably going to dinner with Grace right after. But we hadn't spoken since yesterday, and since I didn't see her in school and since she didn't respond to my texts after school, I started thinking I might not hear from her.

"Hey, Swade," Dad says as I walk into the kitchen.

He and Mom are sitting across the table from one another. Dad's eating a bowl of the chili Mom brought home from the coffee shop. Mom's thumbing her phone.

"I'll be out front," I say.

"What?" Mom looks up.

"I need to talk to Zoey." I wave my phone and head for the door. "I'll be on the steps."

"It's dark," Mom says. "Why can't you—"

"It's fine, Erica," Dad says.

I'm out the door before Mom responds, and a few seconds later, I'm on the front steps leading up to the walkway of our building calling Zoey.

"Why are you calling me?" she answers.

"Hey, Zoey," I say.

"Why are you calling?"

"Because I—"

"Haven't you ever heard of FaceTime?"

"I'm outside," I say. "No Wi-Fi."

"Gil and Erica let you go outside by yourself?"

"I know, right?" I smile. "I didn't want anyone barging in on our conversation."

"Barge, barge, barge!" Zoey says. "So why didn't you text?"

"I didn't want to text this conversation."

"Oh."

"You understand, right?"

She pauses. "Uh-huh."

"So how was robotics?" I ask.

"Our robot finally looks like a robot," she says. "It's so good."

"You're going to kick some bot butt!"

"I hope so."

"I know so."

I reach down and flick away a pebble caught between my toes. I'm wearing my favorite flip-flops, the black-and-white pair I got for my birthday, the same ones Malik has. We always put on our flip-flops after games and practices. Malik has the hairiest toes, and for the last few weeks, his right big toenail has been all black and blue and yellow because he jammed it doing a backflip.

"It's so weird," I say. "Now that I've told you, I feel so much lighter. More bouncy."

"You more bouncy?" Zoey laughs. "Impossible!"

"I know!" I laugh, too. "But I do. I feel lighter and looser. It's like I was holding my breath for all this time but didn't realize it."

"Dolores says hey."

"She's there?" I say. "Zoey, I don't—"

"Relax. She just walked in."

"I can't relax. Where are you?"

"The kitchen. Eating ice cream."

"Sea salt caramel?"

Zoey laughs again. "I finished the sea salt caramel as soon as you left," she says. "Strawberry cheesecake."

Suddenly, it's yesterday afternoon, and I'm back at Zoey's kitchen table, and we're eating sea salt caramel ice cream, and she's asking me questions. She wants to know when I first knew, and I tell her I always knew I was different. When she asks what I mean by different, I try to explain but can't. I tell her I only started figuring out what different was last year, and when she asks me how I started figuring it out, we say "YouTube" at the same time.

I tell her all about the videos I've been watching of kids sharing their coming-out stories, and how the videos have helped me so much because the kids in the videos are saying what I'm thinking and are feeling the same things I'm feeling, the exact same things. I tell her there are other kids out there just like me, lots of other kids out there just like me.

"Can I ask you something?" Zoey says.

"Sure," I say.

"How do you know?"

"You asked me yesterday," I say. "I told you."

"I know, but are you sure?"

"You don't believe me?"

"Of course I believe you."

I rub my eye with my palm. "It's not the kind of thing I'd make up, Zoey."

"I know."

"Please believe me."

"I do."

I let out a breath. "You think I'm overreacting."

"I know you're not."

"I'm not overreacting. I don't want kids to find out."

"No one's going to find out, Silas."

I wipe both eyes with my palm. This is why I wasn't sure Zoey was going to text me. Something felt weird yesterday between us. I know it's not every day you tell your best friend you're gay, so things probably should feel weird, but this was something more. I know Zoey. I'm not imagining it. I know she said she was fine with it—and she said that a bunch of times—but I know at least a part of her didn't know what to do with what I was telling her.

"Can I tell you something else?" I say.

"Of course."

"Do you know what Dear Teen Me letters are?"

"No."

"It's when grown-ups write letters to their younger selves and give advice and stuff," I say. "Some of the kids talk about them in their videos, so I started reading them. And once I did, I couldn't stop, because some of them felt like they were written to me."

"Cool," she says.

"That's when I started promising myself I was going to do something about this, that when I started middle school, I was going to tell someone. But every time

I started to or wanted to, I couldn't get myself to do it, because once you do, you can never go back. There are no backsies and—"

"Backsies, backsies, backsies." Zoey laughs.

I breathe. "I couldn't get myself to do it, and when—"

The door to the building flies open, and Ms. Perkins and Rex, our upstairs neighbor and her chocolate Labrador retriever, come rushing out.

"Someone's gotta go!" Ms. Perkins says as Rex pulls her down the front walk. "Coming through, coming through."

I slide across the step out of their way.

"Thank you, Silas. Thank you, Silas."

"No problem." I wave.

They charge past and head for the first tree at the end of the walk, the one with the small PLEASE DON'T PEE ON ME sign nailed to it.

Ms. Perkins looks back and shrugs. "When you gotta go, you gotta go."

"What was that?" Zoey asks.

"My neighbor and her dog," I say. I take another breath. "So when Ms. Washington gave us the assignment, that was it. I was done making excuses. That's why I did my presentation on Glenn Burke."

"But you didn't say anything about him being gay."

"I did my presentation on a gay guy, Zoey. A gay baseball player!"

"No, you did your presentation on the guy who invented the high five," she says. "Nobody knew he was gay."

"But kids could find out."

"Right." Zoey laughs. "As soon as you finished, everyone ran off to research Glenn Burke."

"Not funny," I say.

"Connor and Nolan are having a Googling Glenn Burke party at this very moment. Half the sixth grade is there." She laughs again. "You understand middle schoolers so well, Silas."

"I do." I wipe my eyes again. "Getting up there in front of everyone like that was the hardest thing I've ever done. You have no idea."

"I know," she says. "Listen, Silas, I really need—"

"Can I tell you one more thing?" I ask.

Zoey pauses. "Sure."

"You know how I told you I always felt different?" I say. "Well, I feel even more different now. I really feel like one of the queer kids in those videos."

"Queer?" Zoey laughs.

I don't laugh. "Yeah, queer," I say. "That's the word a lot of the kids in the videos use to describe themselves."

"But you say the word *gay*. That's the first time you've ever used that word."

"*Queer* means you're not straight."

"Queer, queer, queer."

I close my eyes. I'm not imagining it. Zoey doesn't know what to do with everything I'm telling her. I know it's weird for her. It has to be. How can it not be? It's weird for me, differently weird.

"Listen, Silas," Zoey says. "I really do need to finish my math homework."

"Yeah, I need to head back inside," I say. "You promise you won't say anything to anyone?"

"You know I won't."

"I know, but promise me again."

"Promise."

10

LIGHTER AND LOOSER

"Start us off, Silas," Webb says, swinging his arms and clapping from the third-base coach's box. "Show them how we do, Number Three."

I'm so amped up stepping to the plate right now that it feels like my feet are coming out of my cleats. I'm always pumped before the first pitch of a game, especially when I'm batting leadoff and especially when it's the first game of a doubleheader. But it's never felt like this. I'm feeling lighter and looser.

I go through my batter's box routine—brushing the

number three on my sleeve, adjusting my left wristband, fixing my helmet, tugging the bottom of my jersey, rotating the bat twice, tapping the plate—outside corner, then inside corner to make sure my distance is correct—three half swings, and then bouncing the bat off my shoulder and bringing it about my head. And the whole time I'm going through my routine, I'm smiling at the Thunder's pitcher. I'm never smiling like this, and I can see that he has no idea what to make of it.

The pitcher's a lefty, and I love facing lefties because I see the ball so much better leaving a lefty's hand. It's not that I don't see the ball well leaving a righty pitcher's hand, but when it comes to lefty pitchers, I own them.

I know Thunder Pitcher's starting me off with a fastball. He likes to start every batter with a fastball. I faced him once last year, and I also watched him throw an inning a couple of weeks ago before our games against the Fury. He thinks he can blow everyone away, but he can't blow me away. If his first-pitch fastball is where I want it—low and over the outside corner of the plate—I'm swinging hard, making contact, and driving the ball.

"Renegades are ready," Webb says. "Renegades are ready."

I'm laser-locked, focused on the ball in Thunder Pitcher's left hand as he winds up and delivers the pitch . . . right where I want it.

I swing harder and faster than I ever have. When my bat meets ball, the ball takes off like a missile toward right field, and I take off for first like a Thoroughbred exploding from the starting gate. As I race down the line, I watch the right fielder run back and back and back as the ball keeps going farther and farther and farther than I've ever hit a ball.

I've never led off a game with an over-the-fence home run, and I've never hit an opposite-field, over-the-fence home run . . . until now.

"Pow!" I spring off first base. "Pow, pow!"

I run full speed to second with my fist in the air. When I make the turn, I look back toward home plate, and for a blink, I see Glenn Burke in the batter's box, wearing his number three Los Angeles Dodgers uniform and blasting his first-ever major league home run off the hardest-throwing pitcher in baseball.

My arm's still up as I head for third. When I spot

Webb, I see his hand's out to shake mine, but when he sees that my hand is up, he raises his.

"Pow!" I give him a leaping high five without breaking stride.

"That's how we do, Number Three!" Webb cheers.

I sprint for home. Malik's the on-deck batter, and he's waiting for me at home plate, dancing with his mouthguard dangling out of his mouth. I raise both arms, and he raises both of his, and when I cross the dish, we do a jumping double high five.

"Pow!" we say.

I'm standing on our bench in the dugout shaking out my legs. Webb's right next to me with one foot up on the end of the bench and his arm draped across his knee.

"Show them how we do, Twenty-Five," Webb says. "Get us going again."

Ben-Ben wears number twenty-five, and he started our three-run rally last inning by ripping a double into the left-field corner. We're up 5–2 in the fifth, and he's at the dish with one out and nobody on.

"Let's go, Ben-Ben," I say.

"Why Ben-Ben?" Webb asks. "Why not just Ben?"

"Because he always says things twice," I say, jumping up and down.

"Never noticed."

"Oh, you will now."

Webb's in the dugout instead of coaching third because he still wants to be around the players in the game during the game like he was when he was an assistant. So for an inning or two every game, he lets Coach Noles take third.

"Good eye, Twenty-Five," Webb says as Ben-Ben takes a low pitch for ball one. He blows on his hand and then taps my leg. "Watch him dig in with his front foot. Coach Rockford and I had him make that adjustment."

"I do that," I say. "For traction. So I don't skid."

"It's helping him focus and stay in rhythm," Webb says. "It's all about rhythm and timing at the plate; you know that. A few milliseconds is the difference between a home run and a foul ball."

"Milliseconds," I say in my deep Webb voice. "A hitter has only milliseconds to analyze a pitch, decide what to do, and then follow through with his hitting plan." I swing my arms and clap. "Hitting is all about timing."

"Mock me all you want, Number Three." Webb playfully knuckle-punches my shoulder. "But you know as well as I do timing's the reason you've been finding the sweet spot all year."

Webb's the one who's taught me all about the sweet spot. It's where you want your bat to meet the ball, the spot where the optimum amount of energy gets transferred.

"Wait for yours, Ben-Ben," I say as he fouls the second pitch into the dirt. "Wait for yours."

Webb blows on his hands and shakes out his arms. "I'm done with the cold already," he says. "I need me some baseball weather." He tucks his hands into the pouch of his Renegades hoodie. "Go ahead, Number Three. Let's hear it."

I pat my chest and smile. "Baseball weather is when you know baseball season has finally arrived," I say in my Webb voice again. "The chill's gone from the air, even when the sun peeks behind the clouds." I rub my arms and then jump up and down like I'm trying to keep warm. "I live for baseball weather."

I do live for baseball weather. Most kids get drained on hot days, but not me. I'm the solar-powered kid who loves it when it's scorching hot. For me, the hotter the better, because the hotter it gets, the hotter I get.

"Way to be patient, Twenty-Five," Webb says as the next pitch to Ben-Ben sails wide for ball two. "I'm so impressed with Ben this season."

"Ben-Ben," I say, still smiling.

"Ben-Ben," he says. "I'm so impressed with the work he's put in. He's been raking the ball all year."

Raking means you're hitting the ball well—hitting it hard and to all fields.

"Did you know Ben-Ben's been learning about the physics of hitting a baseball?" Webb asks.

"He's in a robotics club," I say.

"Yeah, he designs and builds robots. Amazing. I for one had no idea he was so into science."

"My best friend Zoey's in a robotics club," I say. "She's amazing at programming."

Ben-Ben swings at the next pitch and smokes a hard ground ball past their first baseman into right field for a base hit.

"Pow!" I leap off the bench. "Way to go, Ben-Ben."

"Great piece of hitting, Twenty-Five." Webb pumps his fist. "That's how we do."

I grab the fence with both hands and shake it. "Should've had that, Rodriguez," I shout to the Thunder's first baseman.

He turns and waves his glove at me. Then he takes out his mouthguard and smiles.

"You're no Benjamin Franklin Rodriguez!" I add.

Whenever we play the Thunder, I'm always saying things from *The Sandlot* to their first baseman because his last name is Rodriguez, just like the character from the movie, except his first name is Joseph, not Benny. He knows I'm only kidding, and Webb knows it, too, which is why I'm saying something to a player on the opposing team while standing next to him.

Webb loves *The Sandlot* almost as much as I do.

I inhale a deep breath and spit a sunflower seed at the dandelion in front of me. It brushes the tip of its leaf. I inhale another breath and spit a second seed—this one bull's-eyes the flower.

"Pow!"

Whenever I'm playing center field, I always keep a

wad of seeds in my cheek and spit them at patches of grass, divots, pieces of paper, and dandelions.

"Let's go, Brayden," Malik says, pounding his glove at short. "Rock 'n' roll."

"Rock 'n' roll," I say, imitating Malik.

Without looking back, he smacks his butt with his glove.

We're up 9–5, and the Thunder are finally down to their last out. We were up by seven heading into the inning, but Brayden gave up three runs and four hits before recording an out. Webb brought him in to pitch the final frame, but by the way he trudged to the mound, I knew he didn't want to throw. But now we're an out away from winning the game, completing the double-header sweep, raising our record to 7–1, and extending our first-place lead to two full games.

"Except for Rodriguez," I shout at the Thunder's first baseman, who's at the plate, "you're all an insult to the game!"

I've said that line from *The Sandlot* every time the Thunder's first baseman has been up this afternoon, and even though Webb is probably tired of it, I have to keep saying it because the kid hasn't gotten a hit all afternoon. And in baseball, when something's working, you keep on doing it.

I'm up on the balls of my feet and pounding my glove. I know exactly what I'm going to do if the ball is hit to me and exactly what I'm going to do if the ball is hit elsewhere. My eyes are laser-locked on Brayden's hand right as he rocks into his windup and delivers the pitch.

Inside, ball one.

"Jase!" I call to our third baseman. "A little to your left."

Jason raises his glove and takes a couple of steps toward short.

"A little more off the bag," I call to Luis at first.

He takes a half step to his right.

A center fielder has the whole field in front of him and can see things the other fielders can't, so good center fielders are constantly calling out directions. Webb's told me he loves it when I do.

I run my tongue along the side of my cheek that doesn't have the wad of seeds. It feels a little raw because that's where I kept them during the first game, and all the salt does that. I tongue a seed out of the other cheek and spit it at the same dandelion, and once again, I bull's-eye it.

Rodriguez fouls Brayden's next pitch toward the bleachers behind our dugout.

"Incoming!" Malik's mom cries. "Incoming!"

Malik hides his face in his glove.

Whenever a foul ball's hit toward where the Renegades parents sit, Malik's mom always shouts, "Incoming," and each time she does, Malik covers his face. Every team has that one over-the-top, loud parent, and for the Renegades, it's Ms. Andrews. At least she doesn't have her cowbell today—Malik made her leave it in their car. Malik didn't mind his mom carrying on like she does nearly as much when Brayden's dad was still in the bleachers because he used to be just as over-the-top and loud. But now that he's assistant coach, she's all by herself, and it's much more noticeable and much more embarrassing.

I never have to worry about that with my parents. They're not loud cheerers. And they don't come to my games as much anymore. When they do, they never stay the whole time. Today they didn't get here until the third inning of the opener, so they missed my leadoff home run. But they did see me single-handedly manufacture a run in the next inning when I beat out a grounder to third for an infield single, stole second, stole third, and then came around to score on a wild pitch. And in the fifth, they saw me make a sliding catch in short right and then double off the runner at first. But by the sixth inning, they were gone. Dad had to take Haley to gymnastics, and Mom had to pick up Semaj at occupational therapy.

"Close it out, Brayden!" I shout. "Shut the door!"

"Finish him off!" Luis pounds his glove.

Rodriguez fouls Brayden's next pitch into the dirt, and now we're one strike away from completing the sweep.

All the Renegades are chattering.

"Let's go, Brayden!" Ernesto shouts from left field.

"One more, one more!" Ben-Ben claps at second.

"Rock 'n' roll, Brayden," Malik says.

I pound my glove and stare at the ball in Brayden's hand. Sometimes I know when the ball's coming my way. Of course, I can't know for sure, but sometimes I get this feeling that it is, and a lot of the time, that feeling is right. As I watch Rodriguez set himself at the plate, I have that feeling.

Brayden rocks into his windup, and as soon as the

ball leaves his hand, I see that the pitch is tailing off the plate. Rodriguez swings at the chaser, makes contact, and swats a sinking line drive over Malik's head into short left-center. But since I'm moving with the pitch, I have a great jump on the ball, and on the dead run and with my glove fully extended, I snag the ball backhanded and knee high.

"Pow, pow!" I leap into the air.

I'm still running full speed toward Malik, and we flying-chest-bump.

"Pow!" we shout at the same time and then crash to the ground.

All the Renegades pile on.

THE STORY OF LAMONT SLEETS

When Ms. Washington gets all excited about a lesson, she gets real theatrical and starts speaking in this dramatic, booming voice like she would if she were on a stage. That's exactly what she's doing right now.

"I'm feeling so inspired this afternoon." She walks to the middle of the room with her fists clenched next to her ears and then opens her hands and raises them over her head. "You've all inspired me so." The bottom of her light green sundress flows as she spins around. "And I want to hold on to this feeling for as long as I possibly can."

Zoey and I are sitting on one of the large plaid floor pillows in the graphic novel corner. Zoey's hand is cupped over her mouth, but not enough to hide her grin, and my hand's around my eye so I can't see Zoey sitting on my left, because if I could see her, I'd lose it.

I thought it was going to be weird seeing Zoey today. I hadn't seen her since her house last Wednesday, which is the longest we've gone without seeing each other all year, except for during Christmas, when she visited her aunt in Cincinnati. But when she walked into ELA a few minutes ago with Mia and Kaitlyn and made like nothing's changed even though everything's changed, it wasn't weird at all.

"How will I hold on to this feeling?" Ms. Washington crosses her hands over her chest and starts to pace, taking deliberate steps. "For one thing, I'm going to use it to fuel our lessons and power our learning." She's looking down as she speaks. "And these lessons and this learning will be rooted in what all of you brought to this classroom these last few weeks."

The first time Ms. Washington got all theatrical like this back in September, pretty much everyone busted out laughing. Zoey's sister Grace says that's what happens every year. It happened when she had Ms. Washington. But you get used to it really quickly because you don't have much of a choice. Still, there are times—like now—when it's next to impossible not to smile, and the smiling is contagious, and then so is the cracking up.

"Your oral presentations will be our springboard, our springboard toward discovery and greater understanding." She stops pacing and looks up. "Each afternoon this week, we'll be focusing on a different individual, an individual that you believed was worthy of introduction to your classmates."

Considering how often we all see Ms. Washington get theatrical like this, it's pretty lame that we still have trouble controlling ourselves. Not only does Ms. Washington direct the shows up at the high school, but she also stars in most of the productions at the Playhouse. Two years ago, she was Belle in *Beauty and the Beast*, and last year she stole the show as Audrey in *Little Shop of Horrors*. From what Grace says, Ms. Washington really wanted to be in *Bye Bye Birdie*, but she has an out-of-town wedding the opening weekend and would've missed half the performances.

"Together, we're going to deep dive." She uncrosses

her hands and holds them out, palms up and fingers spread. "Together, we're going to learn more about these individuals, and maybe that will inspire one or some of you to deep dive on your own and learn more about an individual who interests you. Now let us begin our journey."

Ms. Washington lowers her hands and reaches into her back pocket. She pulls out a baseball cap—a Los Angeles Dodgers baseball cap—puts it on, and faces me.

"Today we deep dive and discover Glenn Burke."

I can't breathe. It feels like a cinder block is pressing against my chest, and by the way Zoey's looking at me, I know I'm turning white or red or that my face has absolutely no color. Zoey has this blank look on her face— this blank, helpless look—like she knows what's about to happen, and there's nothing she can do to stop it. There's nothing I can do to stop it either, but it has to stop.

"Ever since Silas shared his story," Ms. Washington says, still looking at me, "Glenn Burke has been on my mind. Why has he not gotten credit for inventing the high five? Why has he not gotten credit for inventing the world's most famous handshake?"

She knows. Ms. Washington's figured it out. She

can't say that she knows. This can't be happening. This can't be happening. This can't be happening.

"Maybe Glenn Burke hasn't gotten credit," she says, "because maybe Glenn Burke *didn't* invent it."

I reach for Zoey's stainless-steel water bottle and down at least half of it. Then I close my eyes and try to will the air back into my lungs.

"Permit me to tell you a story." Ms. Washington drags her stool to the back of the class and sits. She waits for everyone to face her. "Permit me to tell you the story of one Lamont Sleets Sr. In the late 1960s, nearly a decade before Glenn Burke raised his hand and *invented* the high five, Lamont Sleets Sr. was a soldier serving valiantly in the Vietnam War, as a member of the First Battalion, Fifth Infantry, a unit better known by their nickname, the Five."

I know what Ms. Washington's doing. She's creating drama, building tension, and preparing to expose the truth, the whole truth. She can't do this to me. She can't do this to me. She can't do this to me.

"A year after the Five returned from Vietnam," Ms. Washington says, clasping her hands in her lap, "a reunion was held at the home of Lamont Sleets Sr. When the soldiers marched through the front door, Lamont Sleets Sr. welcomed them with their signature greeting."

Ms. Washington looks back at me. She has to see me gripping—squeezing—the water bottle with both hands. She has to see the beads of sweat on my forehead, the beads of sweat dripping down my temples onto my cheeks. She has to see me trembling.

"Five!" Ms. Washington stands. She raises her hand and spreads her fingers wide. "As the band of brothers reunited, that's what they all shouted with their hands held high. Five!" She looks around. "Now, Lamont Sleets Sr. had a son, Lamont Sleets Jr. At the time, he was a mere toddler, and when the little lad witnessed this, he insisted on joining in. He jumped and slapped his tiny palm against each and every one of their man-sized hands."

I know the Lamont Sleets story. I learned about it when I was researching Glenn Burke.

"High five!" Ms. Washington says in a child's voice. "That's what the little lad yelled." She walks deliberately to the middle of the room and then turns to me again. "High five."

"No," I say, surprising myself that I'm capable of forming a word. "No, that's not—"

Ms. Washington holds out her hand. "Let me tell you about Lamont Sleets Jr. That little lad turned into quite the athlete. As a young man, he earned himself a scholarship to play collegiate basketball for the Racers of Murray State University. At his very first practice, he greeted his new teammates with high fives." She snaps her fingers. "In an instant, the high five became the Racers' handshake, and when the players on the other teams saw this handshake, they started doing it, too." She sits back down on her stool. "That's the true origin story of the high five."

"No." I shake my head. "It's not. That's not true."

Ms. Washington looks around the room but doesn't say anything. Then she smiles. "Silas is right," she says. "It's not true."

"I don't understand," Nolan says. "It sounds true to me."

"It's not," Ms. Washington says. "The origin story I just shared with you is pure fiction, a hoax."

"A hoax?" Kaitlyn says. "Why would someone do that?"

"That's a great question." Ms. Washington smiles again. "Why would someone do that?"

Ms. Washington looks back at me. She wants me to answer. She knows I know. But I can't answer and won't, because if I do, everyone . . .

"Perhaps for attention, perhaps as a joke," Ms. Washington says. She holds out her hands. "Perhaps because they knew they could get away with it."

"So they lied," Kaitlyn says. "They stole someone's truth."

"It appears they did," Ms. Washington says. "They stole someone's truth."

"How can they get away with that?" Connor asks.

"I have my theories," Ms. Washington answers.

Zoey rubs my arm, and when she does, it only makes me more anxious because I know everything I'm feeling right now—fearing right now—is for good reason. A droplet of sweat falls from my chin and lands on my wrist.

"Sadly, lies will often drown out the truth," Ms. Washington says. "Glenn Burke doesn't get the credit he deserves because a lie drowned out the truth, his truth."

"How could that happen?" Connor asks.

"We live in a time where the difference between fact and fiction, the difference between truth and untruth, is more difficult to discern than ever. Far too many are far too quick to believe anything and everything they hear." Ms. Washington clasps her hands in her lap again. "We can no longer allow that to happen. Because it's dangerous, harmful, and unfair. It's up to you—it's up to us—to seek out the truth, to spread the truth, and to fight for the truth."

I'm staring at the splash of sweat on my wrist. I refuse to look up because I know Ms. Washington's looking at me, and the last thing I want to do right now is to make eye contact with her.

"Our truths matter," Ms. Washington says. "Just ask Glenn Burke."

12

WAITING FOR GRACE

"I don't know what I would've done if she'd said something," I say.

"Well, you don't have to," Zoey says. "She didn't."

We're sitting on the low brick wall by the bushes next to the faculty parking lot, which is where we wait for Grace to pick us up every Monday after school. Zoey's swinging her legs like Haley does when we're at the movies and the previews are about to start.

"I'm still shaking." I hold out my hands like I did the other day in her living room. "I really don't know what—"

"You don't have to," she says again. She squeezes my fingers. "Relax."

I look out into the lot. I didn't like it when she told me to relax on the phone the other day, and I don't like her telling me now, but I don't say anything. It's the first time we've been alone since her house, and if I say something, it'll only add to the weirdness I'm not imagining.

"What was Ms. Washington trying to prove?" I ask.

"She wasn't trying to prove anything."

"Why would she do that to me?"

"Silas, she didn't do anything," Zoey says. "You know how Ms. Washington gets."

I do know how she gets. She's one of those teachers who wants you to think and doesn't always give clear-cut answers. She likes to throw out thoughts and ideas and let you try to figure things out on your own. But I have no idea what she was getting at today.

"What if she brings it up tomorrow?" I say.

"She's talking about someone else tomorrow." Zoey stops swinging her legs and checks the time on her phone. "Grace needs to get here already."

"If she'd brought up that Glenn Burke was gay . . ."

I stop and look back at the school to make sure no

one's around, to make sure no one's within a soccer field of our conversation, a conversation I can't believe we're having at school.

"What if . . . what if someone from class decides to look up Glenn Burke?" I say.

"Grrrr," Zoey says. "Silas, are we seriously back to that? No one's going to find out he was gay."

I look back at the school again. "This conversation stops as soon as we see Grace's car."

"Okay."

"I'm serious. We change the subject as soon as we see Grace pull into—"

"Let's change the subject now." She taps my shoulder. "I can't believe my tournament's a week from Saturday. The team has so much we need to do between now and then."

"You'll do it," I say.

"We're naming our robot today."

"Cool." I pick up a twig from the dirt under the bush behind me and trace the cracks in the bricks.

"I have the best name ever for it."

"What is it?"

"I can't say. Not until I convince the eighth graders

that's what we're naming it." She hops off the wall and faces me. "You should tell Grace."

"What?"

"I think you should tell Grace."

"I thought we were changing the subject."

"Grace would—"

"No, Zoey."

She moves in front of me and puts her hands on my knees. "You know she'd be cool."

"Zoey, no. I'm not telling anyone else."

"You know she would be."

"I don't care," I say.

She presses my knees. "I think she knows."

"What?" I drop the twig. "How does she know? What did you—?"

"She asked me one time."

"Asked you?" I feel my heart beating against my chest. "What did you say?"

"I told her no, I didn't think so."

"You didn't think so?" I push away her hands.

"Silas, I never really thought about it until last week."

"I can't believe you never told me this."

"Seriously? What would you have said if I'd told you Grace asked me if you were gay?"

I glance back at the school again. "When was this?"

"Like last year, maybe. I don't know." She puts her hands back on my knees. "Relax, Silas."

I stare but don't say anything.

"Silas, I think . . . I think you might be overreacting. I know I said I didn't think—"

"I'm not overreacting, Zoey," I say. Then I shake my head and then half smile.

"What's so funny?"

"You sound exactly like some of the kids in the coming-out videos," I say. "Some of them talk about how you should find an older person you can trust. They say it in some of those Dear Teen Me letters, too. They say it gives you strength and confidence."

"Zoey Pichardo knows what she's talking about!" She pats her chest and double-dimple grins. "So will you—"

"What the . . .?" I slide off the wall and motion to the gray SUV turning into the lot. "Why's my dad here?"

He's smiling and waving as he pulls into the empty spot reserved for the school nurse. Semaj is waving, too, from her car seat in the back.

"Hi, Swade," he says, lowering the window.

I hold out my hands. "What are you doing here?"

"Hi, Zoey." He waves.

She waves back. "Hey, Mr. Dubs."

Zoey calls my parents Mr. and Mrs. Dubs. Dubs is her abbreviation for W.

"What are you doing here?" I ask again.

He opens the door and gets out. "One of your mother's employees cut herself."

"The new girl?" I say. "Kaila?"

"As a matter of fact, that was the name your mother said."

"Is she okay?" Zoey asks, skipping to the back door.

"They went to urgent care," Dad says.

"Then she's not okay," I say.

"Your mother's erring on the side of caution. You know how she gets."

"But why are you here?"

"What do you mean, why am I here?" He walks around the front of the car. "Your mother said I needed to pick you up."

"No." I make a face. "Grace picks us up on Mondays."

"Beep." Zoey taps Semaj's head. She's next to Semaj in the back seat. "Beep, beep."

Semaj giggles. "Beep, beep." She pats one of Zoey's dimples. "Beep, beep."

"Gentle," Zoey says. "Gentle."

"Zo, Zo." Semaj laughs. "Beep, beep."

"I'm pretty sure your mother said I needed to pick you up at three thirty," Dad says.

"No. Grace is picking us up. Maybe she said something about picking us up next Monday because Grace has rehearsals next Monday."

"No, I'm pretty sure . . . Oh, who knows anymore? I give up." Dad faces the parking lot and rubs his bald spot. "Well, since I'm here already," he says, turning back, "there's no need for Grace to come get you. Text her that I'll—"

"Can't," Zoey interrupts. "She's already on her way. I don't text Grace when I know she's driving."

"Good on you," Dad says. "Good on you." He steps to me. "Your mother was going a mile a minute when she called. Go here, do this, get that. Maybe she did say next week. I have no idea." He's still rubbing his bald spot. "All I know is I'm here, and apparently, I'm not supposed to be."

"Your boss let you out of work?" I ask.

"I told him it was a medical emergency," Dad says. "If he wants to be a jerk about that, let him." He checks his phone. "Let's see. If I understand my orders correctly, I need to pick up Haley and then drop her and Semaj at the Jump & Grind and then . . . You're sure Grace is taking you home?"

"Yeah."

"Well, it does save me a few minutes. Let me get moving." He holds out his fist. "I'll see you at home, Swade."

I give him a light dap. "Later, Dad."

"Later, Mr. Dubs," Zoey says, sliding out of the back seat. "Bye, Semaj."

"Bye, bye." Semaj waves with both hands. "Bye, bye."

Dad checks Semaj's car seat through the window, gets back in the car, and drives off.

Grace turns into the lot as he pulls out.

"Perfect timing," Zoey says.

"That's for sure," I say.

Grace parks her Kia along the curb.

"Did you say anything?" Grace says, hopping out and pointing at Zoey. "If you said anything, I'll be so—"

"I didn't say a word." Zoey holds up her hands. "I swear."

"Say anything about what?" I ask.

"Did she say anything to you?" Grace asks me as she walks around to the trunk.

"I have no idea what you're talking about," I say.

"I didn't say a word," Zoey says, double-dimpling. "No hints, no nothing." She jumps up and down. "Open it, open it!"

"Right on." Grace drumrolls the trunk.

"What's happening?" I ask. "What is this?"

"Here goes," Grace says.

She pops open the trunk and takes out a blue rolling suitcase, the kind that fits into the overhead compartment on a plane. Then she takes out a black one and lays them both on the sidewalk.

"All yours," she says.

"What is this?" I ask.

"Open them," she says.

I unzip the black suitcase, and the second I open it, I know exactly what I'm looking at.

"No way!" I unzip the blue suitcase. "No way!"

"You like?" Grace says, smiling.

"Like?" I say. "Like? This is nuts!"

13

THE *SANDLOT FASHION SHOW*

I'm behind the bleachers in back of the third-base dugout with the blue and black suitcases open on the ground. Theo and Kareem have been spitting sunflower seeds down at me the whole time I've been back here, but it hasn't bothered me at all, because the only thing I care about right now is what I'm about to do. And what I'm about to do is going to be absolutely hilarious.

I knew what was in the suitcases the second I saw the KC Monarchs cap, the exact one Kenny DeNunez wears, and the white button-down baseball jersey with the green trim, the exact one Yeah-Yeah wears. The suitcases contained the clothing the kids wore in *The Sandlot*.

"You almost ready back there?" Webb calls out.

"Just about," I say.

All the Renegades are up on the bleachers getting ready for the start of practice. When I got to Field of Dreams a few minutes ago, I went right to Webb and told him what I wanted to do, and just like I knew he would be, he was down with it, so long as I didn't cut into practice time.

I knew I was going to do what I'm about to do the second I opened the suitcases yesterday.

"How'd you get all these?" I'd asked Grace.

"Perks of my job," she answered.

"This is nuts!" I said at least ten times while jumping in circles and double-high-fiving Zoey and Grace. "This is nuts!"

"These aren't for keeps, Silas," Grace said. "You do know that?"

"Oh, I know," I said, putting on the thick glasses, the ones Squints wears.

"You have to take real good care of them."

"I'll treat them like the treasures they are."

"Rad," Grace said. "I probably won't be able to get these back from you until after opening night because rehearsals are taking over my life this week and next."

"I can't wait for practice tomorrow."

It's practice tomorrow, and I peep my outfit in my phone—an orange-and-yellow striped shirt, baggy khaki shorts, white sneakers, a catcher's mask on top of my head, and a wooden bat resting on my shoulder.

"Let's do this, Silas," I say.

I charge around the bleachers and bolt to the top row.

"My fellow Renegades," I say, holding the bat up high and shaking my hips like I'm doing the floss, which I did everywhere I went when I was in elementary school. "I present to you the *Sandlot* fashion show."

Luis, Ben-Ben, and Malik start banging the bleachers. Luis and Ben-Ben love *The Sandlot* almost as much as I do, which is why I'd told them they were going to love what I was about to do, even though I wouldn't say what it was.

"You're so weird, Silas!" Theo says, laughing and shaking his head.

"I know, right?" Kareem laughs, too. "So weird."

"All righty," I say. I walk the top row like a model

strutting down a runway. "Which one of you can tell me which character from *The Sandlot* I'm—"

"Ham!" Luis shouts.

"You are correct, sir!" I point the bat. "I'm the one and only Hamilton 'Ham' Porter."

"You're killing me, Smalls!" Ben-Ben says Ham's line from the movie and shakes his hands at me. "You're killing me, Smalls!"

All the Renegades are smiling and laughing just like I knew they would be.

"Go, Silas!" Malik says.

I smile at him. "Be right back," I say.

I shield my face from Theo's and Kareem's sunflower seeds as I dart down the bleachers and back around to the suitcases. I quickly change into my next outfit, which is already laid out on the grass, and a minute later, I'm on the top row again, dressed in a different striped shirt, jeans with big cuffs, a plain black cap on backward, and those thick glasses.

"Squints!" Webb calls out. He laughs. "Michael Palledorous, a.k.a. Squints!"

"You're killing me, Webb." I shake my hands at him. "I didn't even get to ask who I was!"

Webb shakes his hands back at me and then jogs out onto the field.

Ben-Ben stands up and holds out his index fingers and thumbs. "The kid is an L-7 weenie," he says, which is my fave Squints line.

Everyone's laughing even harder than I thought they'd be.

"This is so gay, Silas," Theo says, smacking his sides.

"Yeah, you're so gay," Kareem says.

I flinch.

I don't think anyone noticed, because I'm still smiling, and I have to keep smiling because if I don't keep smiling, everyone will notice and then someone will wonder why and no one can wonder why.

"Be right . . . be right back," I say, smiling like nothing happened.

I charge down the bleachers, and when I get to the suitcases, I put my hands on my hips and bend over. I'm trying to catch my breath, but I can't catch my breath. That word never sounded like that before. I hear it all the time like that—at school, out shopping, online, at baseball—but this time it sounded different. It sounded scary.

I change into the next costume, and the whole time I'm changing, I'm tingling and telling myself nothing happened, nothing happened, nothing happened, even though something most definitely happened.

A few seconds later, I'm walking the top row again, and this time, I'm wearing a white baseball jersey with blue sleeves, jeans with even bigger cuffs, a pair of PF Flyers, and a Dodgers cap.

"Even I know this one," Malik says, waving his arms like he's dancing. "Benny!"

"Benjamin Franklin Rodriguez!" Ben-Ben says. "Benjamin Franklin Rodriguez!"

"Benny 'the Jet' Rodriguez," I say, tipping my cap. "That's what they called him when he played for the Los Angeles Dodgers."

I smile at Malik again, but this time, the smile feels . . . I don't know how to describe it.

SO GAY

A few months after Glenn Burke started in center field in the opening game of the World Series, the Los Angeles Dodgers traded their five-tool talent to the Oakland Athletics, the worst team in baseball. Tommy Lasorda, the manager of the Dodgers, who a lot of people think is one of their greatest managers of all time, and Al Campanis, the vice president of the Dodgers, didn't want someone like Glenn Burke in their organization. And when Billy Martin—one of the most popular figures in the game—became manager of the A's, he made it clear there would never be someone like Glenn Burke on his team.

This is so gay, Silas.

Yeah, you're so gay.

I'm sitting in the dark on the bathroom floor. I have been ever since everyone went to sleep, and everyone went to sleep hours ago.

I can't stop hearing the way Theo and Kareem said it. It's the same way kids say it all the time. But I can't say anything, because if I do say anything, kids are going to start talking and asking questions. And I don't want them to start talking and asking questions. They can't start talking and asking questions. They just can't.

I think about what Billy Martin said, what Billy Martin said to the Oakland A's players when he introduced Glenn Burke to the team: *Oh, by the way, this is Glenn Burke, and he's a faggot.*

Even in the dark, I can see the rows of star-shaped stickers Haley has stuck to the vanity's cabinet door. Each sticker has a different drawing. I'm able to make out some of them—flowers, a duck, a baseball, smiley faces, a rainbow.

When Glenn Burke played for the Dodgers, he was

the heart and soul of their clubhouse, but he must've been scared all the time. I know all about how he was angry and frustrated and lonely and heartbroken when he was run out of baseball, but when he was playing, he must've always been so scared.

This is so gay, Silas.

Yeah, you're so gay.

I press my palms against the tiles and stand up. I turn on the water, stare into the mirror, and look for my reflection in the dark.

Other kids go along with it when kids say it. Other kids always go along with it. Not every kid, but the kids who don't go along with it never say anything. They don't stop it. They just sit there silently, because if they do say something, kids might think. Even when they sit there silently, kids might think.

I cup my hands under the faucet and watch as the water pools out and circles the drain.

It's all I think about now. Whenever I catch myself lost in thought, it's what I'm thinking about. I'm thinking about what every kid does and what every kid says and how every kid looks at me.

It's like I'm keeping score.

15

DESTINY'S CHILD

I'm staring at Zoey's front door, and I have been for a few minutes. I never knock or ring the bell because I'm allowed to let myself in. And I know the door's unlocked, but I don't want to go in, because Zoey's going to want to talk about what happened at practice and I really, really don't want to talk about what happened at practice.

She had a robotics meeting this afternoon, which is why she wasn't in ELA and why we didn't talk in school. It's also why I took the bus here by myself instead of riding with her like we always do on Wednesdays. It feels weird—different—being here. It's my first time here since telling her.

Zoey already knows *The Sandlot* show didn't go as planned because I texted her last night, but I didn't go into details. I told her I would tomorrow, but I really, really, really don't want to.

I reach for the knob and pull open the door. Zoey's waiting for me in the living room on the couch, just like I knew she would be.

"So what happened?" she says, patting the cushion and motioning for me to sit. "Tell me everything."

I kick off my sneakers and slide my bag down my shoulders. "Oh, hi, Zoey," I say.

"Hey, Silas." She pats the cushion again. "So what happened?"

"I don't want to talk about it," I say, sitting down.

"Tell me everything."

"No." I shake my head. "I really don't want to talk about it."

"What happened?"

"My dad'll drop off the costumes when he picks me up," I say. I reach behind me for one of the yellow throw pillows with the tassels on the corners and put it on my lap. "They can't stay at the apartment because Semaj keeps wanting to know what's in the suitcases, and that means it's only a matter of time until she opens one, and as soon as she does . . ." I don't finish the sentence. "I can't even look at them right now."

"Have you been moping like this since yesterday?"

I grip the pillow and don't answer.

Zoey's staring at me. I know she thinks I'm overreacting again, but I'm not overreacting and really can't deal with her telling me I'm overreacting.

"Silas, Silas, Silas," she says.

She bounces off the couch and over to the orange-and-blue FC Cincinnati mini soccer ball against the wall in the corner and starts juggling it with her feet. Zoey can juggle a soccer ball hundreds of times, but the only time she does it in the house is when Dolores isn't home, because of the ceramic vase incident in fourth grade and the picture frame incident last year.

"This can't be the only thing we ever talk about," I say. "Since last week, we always end up—"

"Stop." She catches the ball with one hand and holds out the other. "That's so not true," she says. "You came in and said you didn't want to talk about what happened at practice, so we're not talking about it." She drops the ball and starts juggling again. "It's not the only thing we ever talk about."

"Fine," I say. I wrap my fingers around one of the tassels. "Let's just talk about . . . let's talk about something else. Anything else."

"Robotics?" She traps the soccer ball with her heel.

"Fine," I say again.

"Come with me." She kicks the soccer ball into the corner.

"Where are we going?"

We head upstairs, and a few seconds later, we're in Grace's room, only it looks nothing like the last time I was in Grace's room. It doesn't even look like a bedroom anymore because the only piece of furniture left is the red dresser against the wall. On the floor and taking up practically the entire room is a robotics setup. It looks like someone lifted the top off a large pool table, designed a course on it, and dropped it in the middle of Grace's room.

"No way," I say, walking around the setup. "When did this happen?"

"A few weeks ago," Zoey says, double-dimple grinning.

"Where does Grace sleep?" I ask.

"On the couch in the living room. She actually prefers it."

"This is so awesome," I say. "Did you build this?"

"Our team did." She pats the table. "This field mat should actually be on sawhorses or table legs. That's how it is at the rec center, but I keep it on the floor here."

I look around. The framed poster from the Playhouse's production of *Little Shop of Horrors*, signed by the cast and crew, still hangs on the wall above where Grace's bed used to be. "Your silence will not protect you," the Audre Lorde quote, is stenciled in cursive on the wall over the windows. If not for those, I wouldn't know I was in Grace's room.

"Meet Destiny's Child," Zoey says, sliding over to the dresser and picking up the catcher's-mitt-sized robot.

"Destiny's Child?" I say, smiling. "The eighth graders let you name it?"

"The eighth graders loved my name for our mission model. I told them it was our destiny to win the competition, and that this was our child. They thought it was brilliant."

"Did you tell them how much you love Destiny's

Child?" I'm still smiling. "And that you know the words to every song ever performed by Michelle, Kelly, and Beyoncé?"

Zoey double-dimples again. "Well, you know that, and I know that, but they don't need to know that."

"Can I hold it?" I ask.

"Sure." She hands it to me.

"Wow. It's heavier than I thought it would be."

I see robots like this all the time at school, but I've never held one or looked at one this closely. It's all different colors—gray, white, yellow, and red—and has four wheels, two smaller turntable ones in the front and two bigger ones in the back. Between the wheels is a row of ports with wires connected to all different parts.

"Zoey, this is amazing," I say. "Your team's definitely going to win."

"How can you say that?" she says. "You haven't seen the other mission models."

"I don't need to. Destiny's Child has to be the best."

"Silas, you do realize you have no idea what you're talking about, right?"

"How is it powered?"

She reaches over and tilts it up. "Battery pack."

"What's this?" I point to a circle on the underside.

"A color sensor. It sends down a beam and then reads the information. So when DC's driving along—"

"DC?"

"Destiny's Child, DC," she says. "So when DC's driving along, a black line tells it to do something, and a red line will tell it to do something else. Watch."

A minute later, Destiny's Child is following a black line on the field. When it reaches a structure that resembles a silo, it pushes a lever, and the top pops up. Then DC rotates around and follows a red line over to a small cylinder. It picks up the cylinder, brings it over to a large canister, and drops it in.

"This is so awesome," I say.

"So the goal is to have DC perform as many missions as possible in two minutes and thirty seconds. That's how you earn points. The more difficult the mission, the more points you earn."

"DC has to win."

She powers it off and picks it up. "This is the brain," she says, waving her hand over the block section in the middle. "All the programs go in here."

"The programs you write," I say.

"The programs I write."

She puts DC back on the dresser and then turns to me. She stares but doesn't say anything.

"What?" I say.

She's still staring.

"What?"

"I think you should tell Grace," she says.

I stare back.

"I'm serious," she says. "You should—"

"I thought we weren't talking about this anymore."

"I know, but—"

"Zoey, I heard you the other day."

"I'm not saying you need to today or tomorrow, but maybe when she's done with *Bye Bye Birdie,* you can—"

"I heard you," I say.

"I'm the only one who knows, Silas," she says. "It's so weird for me."

"Weird for you?" I clench my fists. "This isn't about you!"

Suddenly, it's silent, and I'm staring at Zoey again, and she's staring back at me again. There's no longer any doubt about the weirdness between us, not that there was any doubt, but now I know beyond a reasonable one that Zoey feels it, too.

I look down and run my hand along the edge of the border wall of the field mat. "So my mom . . . my mom's taking Haley and me to *Bye Bye Birdie* opening night," I say softly, breaking the silence. "We're going to dinner before. You should . . . you should come with us."

"I should," Zoey says. "Dolores was supposed to take me, but she's shooting a wedding on Friday. So we're going Saturday. After the first day of robotics."

"Everything's next weekend," I say. "*Bye Bye Birdie* opens, you have your competition, and I have a triple-header. If I didn't have games on Saturday, I'd definitely be at your competition."

"No, you wouldn't," Zoey says, smiling, but she's not smiling like she usually does.

"Yeah, you're right." I try to smile, too. "No, I wouldn't."

TEAMWORK

I'm out in center field for fly ball practice, and I'm wearing a bright orange wig underneath my Renegades cap. I've had it on since I got to Field of Dreams, and I've been killing it all afternoon—raking the ball during batting practice and catching everything hit my way during fielding practice, and in baseball, when something's working, you keep on doing it.

"Wade!" Coach Noles shouts. "Last one!"

I'm up on the balls of my feet, and my eyes are laser-locked on the feed chute.

Coach Noles is manning the pitching machine by home plate. He's been mixing speeds and trajectories the whole time Brayden, Ernesto, and I have been out here, but so far, I've chased down every ball, and I'm chasing down this one, too.

The ball shoots out, and the instant it appears, I know it's heading for the left center-field fence. I take off full speed because I need to cover a lot of ground if I'm going to catch it, and I'm going to catch it because, when I'm out in center, it's where hits go to die.

I'm gaining ground and getting close to the fence, but that's not going to slow me or stop me. I leave my feet and dive, and with my glove fully extended, I catch the ball in the webbing and hold on as I hit the ground and crash into the base of the fence.

"That's what I demand from my outfield!" Coach Noles shouts.

But I haven't completed the play. I roll over and spring to my feet and then fire a throw to Ben-Ben at third. I aim for Malik—the perfectly lined-up cutoff man—who lets the ball go through, and my two-hop pea hits Ben-Ben's glove right in front of the third-base bag.

"Holy crap!" Brayden races over from left field and

pats me on the back with his glove. "You're a bad man, Wade!"

"Dude!" Ben-Ben has both arms raised at third. "Dude!"

"Epic!" Malik chomps on his mouthguard and pumps his glove at me. "The catch of the year and the throw of the year."

I take off my cap, shake out the orange wig, and then sprint back to my position in center.

"That's what I demand from my outfield!" Coach Noles shouts again. "But you're not done, Wade. Let's see what you really got out there."

It's not like I haven't been showing Coach Noles what I really have out here all practice, but if what I've been showing him hasn't been enough, I'm up for showing more.

The ball rockets out of the feed chute, and this time it's heading for short right-center.

"I got it, I got it, I got it!" I call on the dead run.

Malik at short and Jason at second are both racing back, but Malik veers off because he knows it's the center fielder's ball, and I never give way.

"Mine! Mine!" Jason shouts.

I'm not stopping or slowing. "Me, me, me!" I call.

Jason dives for it anyway, but the ball tips off the end of his glove. At the last possible moment, I somehow manage to hurdle Jason and avoid a full-impact collision. I also manage to keep my eye on the ball—which has changed direction—and with my bare hand, I reach back and snare it. But the toe of my right cleat clips Jason's shin, propelling me into a midair flip. My cap flies off in one direction and the wig in another, and I crash to the ground, landing on my glove, shoulder, and side. I roll onto my back and hold up the ball, still gripped tightly in my hand.

"Savage!" Luis races out from first base.

"Holy crap, holy crap!" Brayden says, charging in from left.

"Absolutely epic!" Malik says as everybody piles on. "The play of the year."

"That's what I call teamwork!" Coach Noles pumps his fist. "That's what I demand from my outfield."

"Bye, guys," I say as Jason gets into Coach Rockford's car. "See you Saturday."

"Later, Silas." Carter waves.

"See ya," Ernesto says

I shake out my wig like a guitarist in a metal band and wave to Jason, Carter, and Ernesto as Coach Rockford drives off. When they turn out of the Field of Dreams parking lot, I look back at Webb. He's doing a sweep of the bleachers and dugouts, making sure no one left anything behind, like he always does after practices.

I sit on the curb and check my phone. Dad was supposed to be here twenty minutes ago. I knew he'd be late, but I didn't think he'd be this late, and I definitely didn't think I'd be the last one to get picked up. I hate that Webb's waiting on me, because I know he has to get to a coaches' meeting, which is why Jason went home with Coach Rockford instead of him.

"Last but not least," Webb says, walking my way. "Looks like Grace is running late."

"No, my dad is," I say. "Grace has rehearsal for *Bye Bye Birdie* tonight."

"The show at the Playhouse?" he says, standing up the equipment bags he was wheeling. "My wife got us tickets. We're going next weekend." He knees my shoulder. "Text Gil. I'll give you a lift."

"I thought you had a meeting."

"You're on the way."

I text Dad, and a second later, I can see he's typing me back. I know his text is going to be the double emoji response he sends all the time—a thumbs-up and praying hands—and that's exactly what shows up on my screen.

"Ready?" Webb tilts one of the bags to me.

I grab my bag from the sidewalk, pop to my feet, and take the handle from Webb.

"That was quite a catch you made at the fence," he says as we head into the lot. "Quite a catch and quite a throw."

I shake the wig out of my eyes. "I'm like a human baseball magnet," I say.

"A human baseball magnet?" Webb laughs. "I like that."

"That's because you said it!"

He laughs again. "That does sound like something I'd say."

"The best fielders are human baseball magnets," I say in my Webb voice. "They attract the ball and are one with the ball."

"Yeah, that sounds like me." Webb nudges me with an elbow.

I glance back at the fields even though I know we're the only ones here.

"Have you . . . have you ever heard of Glenn Burke?" I ask.

"Glenn Burke the baseball player?" he says. "The guy who invented the high five."

"You know about him?"

"Are you doubting my baseball knowledge, Number Three?"

"My bad," I say, smiling.

"Darn right, your bad."

"I just did a report on him for school," I say. "He invented the high five in 1977, but the opening scene of *The Sandlot* takes place in 1962, and when Benny scores after getting out of the pickle, Ham and Bertram give him high fives. That would've been impossible in 1962. It's an anachronism."

"That certainly is an anachronism," Webb says.

I breathe. "Did you know . . . did you know Glenn Burke was gay?"

"I did," Webb says. "But unfortunately, baseball wasn't ready for a gay ballplayer back then."

"Yeah," I say. "I can't wait for Saturday." I jump the

remaining few steps to his SUV. "The trampoline park is going to be nuts."

"It should be a fun afternoon." Webb fumbles for his keys. "I wish the Renegades had more time to do non-baseball things together. It's how you really get to know one another and become a team." He smiles and imitates my voice: "The trampoline park is going to be nuts."

Webb pops open the back and slides the equipment bags in. I toss my bag on top. Then I take off my wig and chuck it in.

"Webb, I'm gay."

I want the words back the second I say them, the second I hear them out loud. I don't know why I said it, why I blurted it out.

Webb's not facing me, so I can't see his reaction, and I don't want to see his reaction. I just want to undo what I just said, what I just did.

But I can't. There are no backsies.

17

OUT IN THE FIELD

Webb turns but doesn't say anything, and just like I needed Zoey to say something the other day when I told her, I need Webb to say something, anything.

"That must've been incredibly difficult," he finally says.

I try to nod but can't.

"Silas?" he says.

I still can't.

"Silas?" He puts his hand on my shoulder and smiles.

I breathe. But I'm shaking now, like I did when I told

Zoey, and I know Webb can feel it because he's gripping my shoulder and squeezing. His hand feels like Zoey's hug the other day.

"It's okay, buddy," he says.

"Please don't tell anyone."

My first words, and when I say them, tears stream down my cheeks.

"I won't tell anyone," he says.

"Please don't, please don't."

"Silas, I'm not telling anyone."

"Not even my parents."

"Not even your parents," he says. "It's not my place."

I wipe my eyes with my palm and take short breaths. "Only my friend Zoey knows."

"Okay." He's still squeezing my shoulder.

"Promise me you won't—"

"I promise," he says. "I'm not telling anyone." He leans in and looks me in the eye. "But don't underestimate your parents, Silas. They're good—"

"Please don't say anything, please don't—"

"Silas." He smiles, then laughs. "I'm not; I won't. All I'm saying is, don't underestimate them." He lets go of my shoulder. "Grab your glove. Let's go have a catch."

"But what about . . . what about your meeting?"

"Grab your glove, Number Three." He motions to my bag. "Let's go have a catch."

"That was a pretty brave thing you just did, buddy," Webb says, catching my throw. We're out in center field under the lights that went on halfway through practice. "I want you to know, it doesn't change a thing."

I nod.

"I mean it, Silas. Not with me, not with the Renegades. Nothing's changed."

I scoop his low throw on a short hop.

"Nice pick," he says. "Nothing's changed. You'll still never give away an at bat; you'll still never concede an out." He catches my throw and wags his glove. "And you'll still sprint in from center when I go out to the mound."

"Yeah," I say, trying to smile.

I didn't know Webb noticed that I ran in from the

outfield every time he went out to talk to one of our pitchers. I never used to do that with Coach Trent, but I do with Webb.

"Brayden didn't want to pitch that last inning on Saturday," he says.

"I know," I say. "I could tell."

He backhands my throw and fires it right back. "Coach Noles wasn't happy I sent him out there to mop up."

"There's no such thing as mop-up," I say, which is something Webb often says.

"There's no such thing as mop-up." Webb nods. "You know that, and I know that, but not everyone else does." He catches my next throw at his knees and sidearms it back. "Being head coach is a lot different than being an assistant. I knew it would be, but I didn't realize it would be this much of a balancing act. You want everyone to be happy all the time, but it's not possible."

I wind up like a pitcher and throw a curveball that doesn't break. Webb has to jump to catch it.

"Is it hard having your nephew on the team?" I ask.

Webb pauses in the middle of his throwing motion. "Not as hard as it was for Coach Trent having his son on the team," he says. "Jason's not one of our best players; you know that. He's a role player. But when he's your son, you want him . . . It's a balancing act."

I catch Webb's throw with two hands against my chest and hold it there. I close my eyes, and for a moment, I listen to the sounds of the park—the hum of the lights down the foul lines; the clicking of the water sprinklers on the next field; the lowering of the metal gates at the concession stands; the steady, low roar of the traffic on the road beyond the parking lot. I open my eyes, and suddenly, I feel like I'm standing on a movie set, like I'm an actor playing a role, because this doesn't feel like my life, because this can't possibly be my life.

But it is. It is.

"When the Dodgers . . . when the Dodgers found out Glenn Burke was gay," I say, "they traded him to the Oakland A's."

"Yeah," Webb says. "I don't think Tommy Lasorda was the most open-minded individual. He was the manager of the Dodgers at the time."

"I know who he was," I say, and then add in my Webb voice. "Are you doubting my baseball knowledge?"

He laughs. "My bad."

"Darn right, your bad," I say.

He fires a throw that stings my hand.

"Do you think baseball is ready for someone like Glenn Burke now?" I ask.

"I'd like to think so," he says. "I hope so."

"Me too."

I wind up like a pitcher again, and this time, I throw a fastball right into his glove.

"Here comes my knuckleball," he says, motioning for me to crouch like a catcher. He adjusts his grip and then tosses a wobbling pitch that sails way over my head. "Yikes!"

I chase after it, and from where the ball rolled to a stop, I fire a perfect strike into Webb's glove.

"Nice," he says.

I sprint back to where I was. "Billy Martin was the manager of the Oakland A's when Glenn Burke played for them," I say. "Do you know what he said when he introduced Glenn to the other players?"

"I'm sure it was something awful," Webb says.

"'This is Glenn Burke,'" I say, "'and he's a faggot.'"

"Billy Martin was a broken person," Webb says. He throws another ball that stings my hand. "You can't fix broken people." He points his glove. "You know what a faggot is, right, Silas?"

"A word for gay people," I say. "A slur."

"It sure is," Webb says. "Full stop." He catches my throw and starts walking toward me. "I was always led to believe a faggot is a bundle of sticks."

"A bundle of sticks?"

"A bundle of sticks used for kindling, for burning heretics alive centuries ago."

"Heretics?"

"People who believed things that were considered wrong by society," Webb says. "People whose actions and beliefs went against the church or the establishment."

I swallow. "Is that true?"

"Not sure," Webb says. "But I am sure it's a vulgar term, and the way Billy Martin used it was unforgivable. People like Billy Martin are the reason Glenn Burke never got the high five he deserved."

I hold up my glove. Webb smacks it with his.

"I miss talking baseball with you, buddy," Webb says.

"I miss talking baseball with you, too."

"I know we still do, but not like we did when I was

an assistant." Webb motions to the parking lot, and we start walking. "Can you keep a secret?"

"I hope so," I say. "I'm kinda sorta asking you to keep a pretty big one, right?"

"Fair point." Webb laughs. "Do you know why I let Coach Noles take an inning or two at third every game?"

"Yeah," I say. "So you can be in the dugout with the players in the game during the game."

"And it helps keep Coach Noles happy." Webb nods. "But there's another reason."

"What's that?"

"You." He places a hand on my shoulder. "You, Silas. It lets me talk baseball with you. That's how much I miss it."

"Thanks," I say.

"I like strategizing with you. I like it when we dissect pitch counts and discuss game situations. I like talking about where we should position our fielders and whether we should bunt or hit behind the runners. And you know how much I like talking about *The Sandlot*."

"Yeah," I say.

"You be you, Silas Wade, you hear me?"

"Yeah," I say again.

"I'm serious. You be you. Keep being authentic." He rubs my head with his glove. "You have my word that I'm going to do my part ... I'm going to do my part to make sure the Renegades ... that we're the community it should be, the community you deserve. Full stop."

18

TELLING

"Pick up, pick up, pick up," I say.

I'm pacing back and forth on the steps in front of my building. Webb dropped me off a minute ago, and I need to talk to Zoey before I head in.

"Hey, what's up?" she answers.

"Yes!" I say. "Hey, Zoey."

"I only have a second," she says. "I'm still at robotics."

"I didn't want to put this in a text."

"Is everything okay?" she asks. "What's the matter?"

"I told Webb."

"You told—You did? Seriously? Wow, how did it go?"

"I think . . . great," I say. I'm shaking as I speak. "It went great, Zoey."

"Did you tell him in person or on the phone?"

"In person," I say. "At practice just now. We were the only two left at the fields, and . . . and it just came out."

"That's amazing, Silas."

"I know, I know." My voice cracks. "You're not the only one who knows anymore."

"That's amazing, Silas," she says again. "Amazing. I want to hear all about it, but I have to get back to—"

"Webb knew about Glenn Burke," I say. "He knew he invented the high five and that he was gay." I say the last word softly and look around as I do.

"Amazing."

"He said Glenn Burke never got the high five he deserved."

"Silas, I really need to—"

"Go, go, go," I say.

"Thanks. Hey, Silas?"

"Yeah?"

"High five."

19

BEDTIME STORY

"Introducing . . . Glenn Burke!" I say.

I'm standing in the middle of Haley and Semaj's room wearing my Renegades jersey and holding my Wiffle bat. Semaj wouldn't go to sleep after Haley and I finished reading *Croc and Ally*, so in order to prevent a screamathon, I told Semaj we'd read her one more story.

"One mo sto-wee, one mo sto-wee," Semaj says. She's sitting at the foot of her bed swinging her legs. She's been saying the same thing over and over since we put her book back in the night table drawer. "One mo sto-wee, one mo sto-wee."

But Haley didn't want to read Semaj one more story. Haley wanted to make stickers, which is why she's in a split on the carpet with her headphones on and coloring, and I'm about to tell the silly version of the Glenn Burke story. It's the silly version because every story you tell Semaj has to be the silly version, even if there isn't a silly version.

"Here comes the story," I say, tapping the polka dots on the knees of her pajama onesie. "But you have to be quiet."

Semaj covers her mouth and giggles.

Then like I did in Ms. Washington's class, I act out the story of Glenn Burke. For the bases, I use Haley's purple gymnastics hoodie, the dresser, the closet, and Semaj's panda slippers, and when I run around them, I pretend to stumble over Haley's legs because I need to be silly. I don't want to scare Semaj when Dusty Baker hits his home run, so I swing the Wiffle in slow motion. But when I'm Dusty circling the bases, I twirl the bat like a baton and dance, which makes her laugh.

Haley is Glenn Burke, but she doesn't want to be, so instead of greeting Dusty at Semaj's panda slippers for the very first high five ever, she doesn't get up and rolls her eyes when I high-five her.

"Hi fi, hi fi!" Semaj says, waving her hands.

I slide over to the bed and gently high-five her, too.

Then I'm Glenn Burke hitting his home run and silly-dancing around the bases. I high-five Haley again, who still doesn't get up, but this time when I do, I clasp my hands in hers and shake my butt at Semaj.

Semaj squeals.

I jump back to the middle of the room and tell the rest of the Glenn Burke story—how the high five spread through baseball, spread through all sports, and spread all around the world.

"Hi fi, hi fi," Semaj says again, still waving both hands.

I tap them once more.

"That's the story of Glenn Burke," I say. I take off my cap and bow like the performers at the Playhouse. "That's the story of the man who invented the world's most famous handshake."

But just like in Ms. Washington's class, I leave out part of the story—the next part of the story, the most important part of the story, the part of the story I *can't* tell my sisters.

20

BOUNCE! BOUNCE!

I'm in the car with Mom, and we're on the way to Bounce!
Bounce! and I can't remember the last time I was alone
with her like this, and I really, really want to tell her about
Glenn Burke.

I've wanted to tell her about him since we pulled
out of the driveway. We've already talked about Kaila, her
employee who cut herself by accident earlier this week,
about the best places to buy jelly beans and chocolate on
the Monday after Easter, and about how I'm not allowed
to put Peeps in the microwave and watch them explode

anymore because Mom's always the one who ends up having to clean up the mess.

But we haven't talked about what I want to talk about—what I really, really want to talk about—and we're almost at Bounce! Bounce!

So many of the kids in the coming-out videos talk about how telling someone you trust gives you confidence and that you feel relieved and free, but I didn't realize just how much. You can't realize just how much until you do it.

I want to tell Mom that Glenn Burke was gay and that's why he never got credit for inventing the high five. I want to tell her that's why the Dodgers traded him and why the A's ran him out of baseball. And I want to tell her all about what Glenn Burke did after baseball wanted no part of him—how he played for the Pendulum Pirates in the San Francisco Gay Softball League and was voted Player of the Year, how his team played in the Gay Olympics and won the Gay World Series, and how his team played against the San Francisco Police Department in a city league all-star game and beat the police so bad the umps had to call the game.

"We have arrived at your destination," Mom says in

a GPS voice. We pull up to the curb by the entrance. "Here." She hands me a five-dollar bill.

"Thanks, Mom," I say.

"You'll behave yourself in there, Silas?"

"Always do," I say, opening the door and getting out.

"Please don't go too crazy."

I shut the door, and as she lowers the window, I stick my head in, rock it back and forth, and stick out my tongue. She reaches over and swats my shoulder.

"I won't go too crazy," I say.

"Be sure to tell your coaches thank you," she says. "Bringing the whole team here is very generous."

I start backpedaling away. "I will."

"I filled out your waiver online, but I didn't get a confirmation, so if there's an issue, have Webb text me and—"

I turn and sprint for the door.

I duck out of the way just as the bright yellow ball flies past my face.

"Rule number four!" I yell at Brayden. "No head hunting." I point to the sign on the gate to the court. "No head or face shots allowed."

"Rule six!" Brayden points to my foot. "Crossing over the middle line will cause you to be called out."

We're playing trampoline dodgeball, and Ben-Ben and I are the only two left on our team, and Brayden and Malik are the only two left on the other.

"What are you talking about?" I shout. "It's not even touching it!" The tip of my sock is up against the line, but there's no way Brayden can see that from where he is. "And touching isn't crossing!"

Malik runs up the sloped trampoline in the back and does a flip, and when he lands, he spins around and whips his ball at Ben-Ben. It bounces before it hits him.

"Keep showing off." I shake the green ball I'm holding at Malik. "Your time's almost up."

Malik's been doing flips and tricks the whole time we've been here. I knew he was good at gymnastics because he's told me he used to take gymnastics at the place where Haley goes, and I've seen him do front flips and backflips at baseball, but watching him here is nuts.

Ben-Ben bounces up to me at the center line. We each have a ball, but neither Brayden nor Malik does.

Ben-Ben holds the ball in front of his mouth. "On three, we aim for Malik's legs," he says. "One, two, three!"

We both wind up to throw at Malik, but at the last second, Ben-Ben sidearms his ball at Brayden. Malik leaps over my throw, but Ben-Ben's throw hits Brayden on the arm.

"Pow!" I hold up my hand for a high five.

Ben-Ben smacks it hard and then points at Malik. "One down, one to go!"

Malik scoops up a rolling ball and underhands it at me, but it sails by. I hop-skip backward to the side wall and pick it up, and as I bounce next to Ben-Ben, Malik picks up another ball.

"C'mon, Silas!" Malik mocks me as he hops forward. "Rock 'n' roll!"

"You got nothing, Malik." I pump-fake a throw. "Nothing!"

Malik whips his ball at me, but I block it with mine, and the ball goes right to Ben-Ben, who catches it with both hands. Malik's out.

"Champions of the world!" Ben-Ben holds the ball over his head. "Champions of the world!"

"Pow!" I spike the ball. "Pow!"

I bounce over to Brayden, but before I reach him, Malik tackles me. "Dogpile!"

"Rule nine, rule nine!" I shout.

Malik's on top of me and holding me down. He reaches for the ball I spiked and starts pounding me on the head.

"Rule nine, rule nine!" I say, covering my face and laughing. "No shoving, pushing, or roughhousing is allowed."

"Game's over, dude," Malik says, laughing. "There are no rules!"

"Dogpile!" Brayden leaps on top of Malik and me.

"Dogpile!" someone else yells.

Suddenly, the rest of our teammates are bouncing over and jumping on.

"Before we chow down on those wings," Webb says, nodding to the cartons on the table by the door, "we need to talk a little shop." He puts his foot up on the end of the picnic bench and drapes his arm across his knee. "Seven and one heading into the bye week ain't too shabby. That's quite a first half to our season. Now we need to sustain it. No letdowns."

"Renegades are ready!" Theo pounds the underside of the table. "Renegades are ready."

We're all sitting at the two picnic tables in the private party room by the obstacle course. It's the same room Zoey used for her birthday party here in third grade, and the reason I know that is because the *Terminator*, *Jurassic Park*, and *Fast & Furious* video games we're allowed to play for free this afternoon were out-of-date back then and are even more out-of-date now.

"We have two big practices this week and a big triple-header this Saturday," Webb says.

"Renegades are ready!" Kareem bangs the table.

"Those are three winnable games this Saturday," Luis says.

"Every game's a winnable game," I say.

"That's right." Webb points at me. "Every game's a winnable game. We take 'em one game at a time."

"Hear, hear!" Coach Rockford says.

I kick my legs out from under the table and hop onto the bench. "We take 'em one game at a time," I say in my Webb voice.

"Here we go again." Webb shakes his head and smiles. "Time for a Silas impersonation."

I swinging-clap my hands. "We bring our A-game to every game." I step up onto the table. "We do the little things out there. That's what sets the Renegades apart."

"Number Three's working all the baseball clichés," Webb says.

I leap across to the other table, and when I land, Theo and then Kareem try to grab the toe of my sock, but I jump out of the way.

"We have all the right pieces," I say, still speaking like Webb. I pump my fists at the coaches. "All the right parts."

"That we do." Webb swinging-claps.

All my teammates are laughing, and for a moment, it hits me that I really am just like Glenn Burke. Glenn Burke was always standing on the benches in the Dodgers clubhouse and doing stand-up comedy, reciting poetry, and dancing around.

"Number Three, thanks for the show," Webb says. "Now have a seat. We still need to talk a little shop." He holds up his hand.

I leap off the table and high-five it, and when his hand hits mine, he doesn't smack it a little bit harder or hold his look a little bit longer like I thought he might.

"Before we talk a little shop," Malik says, standing, "I have one more announcement."

Webb throws up his hands. "Make it quick, Number Ten," he says.

"This morning, I went for my physical," Malik says, grinning. "I weighed ninety-nine pounds." He points to the cartons on the table by the door. "This afternoon, I shall eat one pound of chicken wings." He raises his arms. "I shall be one percent chicken wings!"

Everyone laughs again.

Webb steps to Malik, gives him a high five, and then presses him back onto the bench.

"Gentlemen, let's talk a little shop." Webb stops smiling. "At last week's games, you refrained from the monkey chants. I didn't acknowledge it, and I should've acknowledged it. I didn't acknowledge it at practices this week either, and I should have. That was wrong of me. Renegades, my apologies. I'm proud of you. Much respect."

"Hear, hear!" Coach Rockford says.

"Now I'm putting a stop to something else," he says. "And it's something I should've put a stop to the first time I heard it." He waves his finger. "The Renegades are no longer saying 'that's gay.' The Renegades will not use that word that way anymore. Full stop."

Everyone's looking at Theo and Kareem because

they were the last ones to say it. And everyone knows they said it to me, and that means everyone's about to look at me. But I don't want everyone looking at me—the last thing I want is everyone looking at me—because if they look at me, they might know, and they can't know.

"Sorry, Webb," Luis says.

"You weren't the one who said it," Ernesto says.

"Hold on, hold on." Webb waves his hand. "Luis, I'm not asking for apologies."

"But I've said it," he says. "I know I have."

"Me too," Ben-Ben says.

Webb waves again. "I don't want apologies," he says. "That's not what I want here. What I want is for us to do better. As a team and as a community, we can all do better." He taps his chest. "That includes me. We shouldn't use that word that way, and we shouldn't tolerate others using it that way. It's homophobic. If we use it or say nothing when we hear it, that's homophobic. The Renegades are better than that. That's the team—that's the community—I want us to be. That's the team I want to be a part of, the one everyone deserves."

I run my finger along a curved groove in the table. I'm trying not to look up, because I don't want anyone's eyes to meet mine, but if I don't look up, someone might notice and wonder why I'm not looking up.

"May I add something?" Coach Rockford raises his hand and steps next to Webb. "The community everyone deserves is a community that respects everyone. The Renegades respect everyone—LGBT, women, immigrants, Muslims, everyone."

"Hear, hear," Webb says, imitating Coach Rockford. He holds out his fist and gives Coach Rockford a dap. Then Webb looks at us. "We can't tell you what to do when you're not here, but what we value here—"

"Webb makes a good point," Coach Noles interrupts. "We can't tell you what to do when you're not here, and we shouldn't. It's not our job."

"I wasn't finished, Coach Noles," Webb says, firmly.

I look up. Everyone's looking at the two coaches.

"I think it's time for wings," Coach Noles says, stepping to the table and patting a carton. "We have four different kinds of sauces. Mild, medium, hot, and blazin'. If you want—"

"I wasn't finished, Coach Noles," Webb says.

"We've talked enough shop, Webb," he says. "Let the boys eat. If you need—"

"I need to finish," Webb interrupts in a tone I've never heard him use before.

My eyes dart from coach to coach. Everyone's eyes are darting from coach to coach.

"This is a baseball team, and these are boys," Coach Noles says. "Your political beliefs—"

"This has nothing to do with politics," Webb interrupts. He's staring right at Coach Noles. "This has everything to do with being human."

Coach Noles waves his hand at Webb and then looks away. "Finish talking shop," he says.

"That's what I intend to do," Webb says. He turns back to us. "These are the rules when it comes to homophobic comments." He puts his foot back up on the bench and drapes his arm across his knee. "These rules apply to everyone—all-stars, relatives, role players, everyone." He raises a finger. "First offense, you're sitting." He holds up another finger. "Second offense, you're suspended. Third offense . . ." He pauses. "Third offense, you're done. Full stop."

21

COACH NOLES AND BRAYDEN

"Gentlemen," I say in my Webb voice, "this is what I call baseball weather." I motion to the sun. "I for one have needed me some baseball weather."

I'm doing my latest Webb impression in front of the bleachers, where Theo, Kareem, Ben-Ben, Luis, and Malik are all getting ready for practice.

"Now we know it's baseball season," I continue. "The chill's gone from the air, and the real hot days—the scorchers—are just around the corner." I swinging-clap my hands. "These are the days meant for baseball."

Theo spits a sunflower seed at me that lands on my arm. I brush it off with my cap and drop the lid into my glove on the bench. Both he and Kareem have been spitting seeds down at me the whole time, but that was the first one to reach me.

"What about this one?" I say, flipping the hair off my face and smiling. "Milliseconds, gentlemen. Baseball is a game of milliseconds. Milliseconds matter running the bases. How many plays are decided by two steps, one step, a half step, fingertips? Milliseconds matter playing the outfield. What kind of jump did you get on the ball? Did you field the ball in throwing position? How quickly did you get the ball out of your glove?"

"Dude, I know you're messing around," Ben-Ben says, "but it's true, it's true."

I place my foot on the bottom bench and drape my arm over my knee. "Who says I'm messing around?"

"It's definitely true in robotics," Ben-Ben says. "Every millisecond counts with some of the missions and tasks. At my competition this weekend—"

"Five minutes, Renegades," Coach Rockford calls to us from the other side of the safety fence. "Five minutes till we stretch."

I slap my lid back onto my head and grab my glove. "We're starting without Coach Noles?" I say. "Coach Noles isn't here yet."

"You haven't heard?" Luis asks.

I sit down next to Malik, who's tying his cleats. "Heard what?"

"How could you not have heard?" Kareem says.

"Because he doesn't go to school with us, tool," Theo says, smacking Kareem with his glove.

"Coach Noles isn't coaching anymore," Malik says. "Brayden's off the team, too."

"Because of what happened at the trampoline park," Kareem says.

"No," Theo says. "It was more than that. Coach Noles and Webb didn't get along."

"I heard Webb didn't like the way he yelled at us," Luis says.

"He didn't yell at us." Malik looks up.

"Not like he did when he was in the bleachers with the parents," Luis says, "but he—"

"I thought they were going to throw down on Saturday," Theo says, punching the air.

"They weren't going to throw down," Malik says. "Coach Noles isn't like that."

"Now we only have two coaches," Luis says.

"And eleven players," Ben-Ben adds. "Eleven players."

I tighten a knot in the webbing of my glove. It never even crossed my mind that Coach Noles would quit the team and pull Brayden from the Renegades. I saw what happened at the trampoline park—we all did—and Webb told me that he and Coach Noles didn't always see eye to eye, but I never thought *this* would happen.

I glance at Malik. He's friends with Brayden. Their families are friends. They live down the street from each other, which is why Malik always rides to practice with them. He knows more about what really happened, and I want to know what really happened, but at the same time, I don't want to know what really happened because—

"So who do you think snitched?" Theo asks.

I flinch like I did last week when Theo and Kareem said what they said to me. But unlike last week, Theo or Kareem or Luis or Ben-Ben or Malik had to have seen this flinch.

"Snitched . . . snitched about what?" I ask.

"About what we said to you the other day," Theo says, motioning to Kareem. "Someone complained to Webb."

"Someone definitely complained to Webb," Ben-Ben says.

I tighten another knot in my glove. I'm the reason Webb said something, but I never said anything. I never complained. He's the one who brought it up, not me.

Theo stands up. "Snitches get stitches," he says.

"Yeah, snitches get snickers." Kareem stands, too.

"Snitches get what?" Theo and Ben-Ben say at the same time.

Kareem's face turns red. "Snitches get . . . snitches get snickers," he says, softly.

"Like the candy bar?" Theo laughs. "Snickers?"

"Where did you get that?" Luis laughs.

"I don't—" Kareem shrugs. "I thought—"

"Snitches get Snickers?" Theo's still laughing. "What does that even mean?"

"Is that what you think people are saying?" Malik asks.

Kareem sits back down. "Yeah, I mean . . . no, I—" His face turns even brighter red.

"Snitches get Three Musketeers." Luis pounds his glove on the bench.

Theo, Ben-Ben, and Malik are all laughing hard, so I start laughing, too. I have to laugh, even though I don't want to laugh, because if I don't laugh, they'll see that I'm not laughing, and if they see that I'm not laughing, they'll want to know why.

"Snickers get Milky Ways!" Ben-Ben says.

Malik stomps his feet. "Snickers get Twix!"

"Hey, Snickers." Theo flicks Kareem's cap off his head. "Why'd you tell Webb?"

"I didn't." Kareem folds his arms and hunches his shoulders. "I didn't snitch."

"Snickers!" Luis pinches Kareem's cheeks. "You're Snickers."

Kareem ducks away.

"Snickers!" Ben-Ben starts to chant. "Snickers!"

"Snickers!" Theo joins in. "Snickers!"

I don't start chanting, and I don't start clapping. And while I'm still smiling and laughing, I really want Kareem to see that I'm not chanting and clapping, because if it wasn't for him right now, everyone's eyes would be on me.

"We said it to you, Silas," Theo says.

"Huh?" I say.

"Kareem and I said it to you." Theo sits down on the bench diagonally in front of me. "Did you say something?"

"No."

"How do we know you didn't?"

"Because I didn't." I take off my cap. "Why would I?"

"Dude, they said it to you," Ben-Ben says. "They said it to you."

"So?" I flip the hair off my face. "I didn't say anything to Webb. Anyway . . . anyway, I have a girlfriend."

"You do?" Malik says.

"Yeah, that girl, Zoey," I say.

"Since when?" he asks.

Suddenly, I'm back in the parking lot with Webb at the moment I told him, and just like then, I want these words back. After hearing them out loud, I *need* these words back, the lie I just blurted out, but there's no possible way to take it back.

"Dude, I didn't know she was your girlfriend." Ben-Ben nudges me in my back with his knee.

"Yeah," I say. "She is."

"Savage!" Luis says.

"Since when?" Malik asks again.

"Since . . . since this year."

Theo pushes my leg with his glove. "Have you kissed her?"

"What do you think?" I say.

"Dude, that's why we're asking." Ben-Ben knees me again. "So what have you done with her?"

"I go to her house every Wednesday, and we're the only ones there," I say. "What do you think we're doing, singing karaoke?"

"Knowing you, yes!" Theo laughs.

"No," I say, wagging my finger and smiling. "We're definitely not singing karaoke."

EVERYTHING'S WEIRD

"Ms. Washington can't be out tomorrow and Friday," Zoey says, waving the remote as she cues up karaoke. "I need her to be in school."

"Need her?" I say.

"Yes, need her. I need her to be inspiring." She slides the remote onto the coffee table. "Grace says that before every performance at the Playhouse, she always gives these inspirational pep talks. I need one for Saturday."

I grab our mics from the shelf next to the modem. "You'll do great, Zoey," I say.

"This is your moment to shine, Zoey Pichardo," she says, leaping onto the couch and imitating Ms. Washington. "This is the moment when all that hard work and dedication pay off. This is your destiny, child." She clenches her fists next to her ears and then opens them and raises her arms. "This is your moment to reach for the stars and shine brighter than the brightest ones in the sky."

"You'll do great, Zoey," I say again. I put the mics by the remote and sit on the edge of the rug. "I know you will."

"Wow, Silas," Zoey says, placing her hands over her chest. "You're all the inspiration I need. Who needs Ms. Washington?" She jumps off the couch. "Thank you so much."

I run my finger along the patterns in the parquet floor pattern, but I don't look at Zoey, because I can't look at Zoey. I didn't have to in school because she missed class for robotics, and on the bus ride here, I looked out the window the whole time. But it won't be long until she says something, because not looking at someone is the type of thing Zoey notices.

"My coach said something to the team," I say.

"About you?"

"About saying 'that's gay' and using the word that way."

"Did he mention you when—?"

"No. Webb would never do that."

She sits down cross-legged on the couch. "It's such a relief you told Webb. I'm so—"

"A relief?"

"Yeah, it is." She picks up the mic. "I didn't like being the only one who knew. It felt so weird."

"Everything about this is weird." I flip my hair.

"What's weird?" Grace says, walking in from the kitchen.

"Hey, what are you doing here?" Zoey says. "I didn't think you'd be home till later."

"Pretend I'm not." She jingles the keys dangling from her rainbow-colored peace sign key chain. "I need to grab a sweatshirt for one of the cast members. Hey, Silas."

"Hi, Grace," I say.

How much of our conversation did Grace hear? Did she just walk in? Or was she waiting and listening in the kitchen? And if she was waiting and listening, what did she hear? Does she know?

"Zoey says everyone's coming to the show on Friday," Grace says. "Dopeness."

"Not everyone." I stop tracing the floor pattern and pick up the remote. "Just my mom and Haley."

"And you and Zoey. That's a solid crew." Grace leans against the couch's armrest. "Sorry things didn't go as planned with the *Sandlot* costumes."

I shrug. "It doesn't matter."

I look up at the TV and start scrolling the titles. I knew Zoey told Grace about what happened at practice because Zoey tells Grace practically everything. I wish she hadn't, and I want to be angry at Zoey for it, but I'm in no position to be angry with Zoey about anything.

"I wouldn't sweat it too much, Silas," Grace adds.

"I'm not thinking about it anymore," I say.

"What aren't you thinking about anymore?" Dolores says, walking into the living room dressed in one of the dark pantsuits she wears to weddings.

"Hey, Mom," Zoey says. "What are you doing here?"

She points to Grace, who's now heading up the stairs. "We had coffee at the Jump & Grind." She gives Zoey a hug and kiss. "When I saw I still had a few minutes before my shoot, I decided to run by the house with Grace for a quick hello." She turns to me and smiles. "Silas!"

"Hi." I wave the remote and manage a smile.

She leans down and hugs and kisses me, too. "How are you doing?" she asks.

"Good," I say. "Good."

"I feel like I haven't seen you at all this week," Dolores says to Zoey. "You've been so busy with robotics, and I've been getting ready for wedding season."

I'm hearing what Dolores is saying, but in my head, her words are being drowned out by all my other thoughts. How long was she in the kitchen before she walked in? Did she hear any of our conversation? Grace had an idea about me—does Dolores have an idea about me? Did Grace say anything to her about me? And what's she going to think of me when she finds out what I said about Zoey? I grip my head. She will find out. Zoey and Dolores talk about practically everything just like Zoey and Grace talk about practically everything.

"Let's go, Mom," Grace says, coming down the stairs with the sweatshirt draped over her shoulder. "I need to get back to the Playhouse." She twirls the peace key chain around her finger and catches the keys. "See you Friday, Silas."

"See you Friday," I say.

"You two have fun this afternoon," Dolores says.

"I'll be able to drive you two again starting Monday," Grace says. "Believe it or not, I actually miss it."

"Of course you miss it," Zoey says, double-dimple grinning. She grabs her mic from the cushion and slides off the couch. "You miss being in the presence of our greatness."

Grace picks up the orange-and-blue mini soccer ball from the floor and bowls it at Zoey.

"Not in the house!" Dolores says as Zoey kicks it back.

She and Grace head out.

Zoey points her mic at me the second the door closes. "For the record," she says, "I only told Grace the *Sandlot* show didn't go the way you wanted. That's it."

"It's fine." I trace the floor patterns with my finger again.

"I wasn't going to lie to her," Zoey says. "She asked me about it, and I told her. But I didn't go into details."

"It's fine."

I look at Zoey, and for the first time all afternoon, we make eye contact, and I know she knows it's the first time we've made eye contact all afternoon.

"One of our assistant coaches quit," I say before she has the chance to say something about it.

"Why?"

"And he pulled his son off the team."

"Why? What happened?"

I breathe. "Because of . . . because of what Webb said to us."

"Really?" She sits back down next to me. "That's horrible. No, that's disgusting."

"I mean, I'm sure there was more to it, but—"

"That's disgusting," she says again. "I'm sorry."

"Why are you sorry?"

"Because I just am. I'm so sorry, Silas."

Zoey's apologizing to me feels like a punch to my gut.

ABOUT GLENN

I'm sitting on the curb in front of our building next to the tree with the PLEASE DON'T PEE ON ME sign. I'm not on the front steps, because if I were on the front steps, someone would see me out of Haley and Semaj's window. Then I'd have to go in, and I'm not ready to go in. Coach Rockford dropped me off after practice, and since it ended a little early, I still have time before I get the text from Mom or Dad asking where I am.

It feels like I'm holding my breath again, like how

it felt before I told Zoey. I didn't realize it felt like I was holding my breath then, but I do now.

At practice today, I wasn't raking the ball to every field and chasing down every ball hit my way. And in the dugout and on the bleachers, I wasn't joking around, imitating my teammates, and keeping everyone loose.

I was thinking about Glenn Burke. I'm still thinking about Glenn Burke. No wonder he was never able to play as well as people thought he would. No wonder he kept getting hurt. All this stuff weighs you down and holds you down and keeps you down. And it weighs you down and holds you down and keeps you down more and more and more with every passing moment.

I press my palms against my temples. I want to know if this is what it felt like for Glenn Burke. I want to know if there were times when he couldn't look his teammates in the eye, because there are times I can't look my teammates in the eye. I want to know if he felt like he was keeping score all the time, because I feel like I'm always keeping score. I want to know if he felt like he was lying all the time, because I feel like I'm lying all the time. What did he say when they asked him if he had a girlfriend? What did he say when they asked him about

172

his girlfriend? He had to say something. He had to make up a story. He had to make up a lie.

I look down at the Wendy's wrapper in the street next to my flip-flop. I think back to last year when the team went to Wendy's. It was on the way back from the tournament in Lakeland, and Webb was our head coach that day because Coach Trent was away on a business trip.

We got there right before they were about to close. There were only two people working, but they stayed open late just for us. Then as we were heading for the door, Webb called us back in. Even though it was after ten and we were dead tired from playing five games and wanted to get home, he made us help clean the restaurant. He said that the two workers were kind enough to stick around and make sure we all ate and that we needed to return the kindness. He told us we weren't leaving until that Wendy's was cleaner than it ever was.

We worked in pairs. I was with Malik. We were in charge of sweeping the floors and bringing the trash out to the dumpster by the drive-thru. But when we got out to the parking lot, we saw that garbage was everywhere. It was so nasty crawling around underneath that dumpster picking up tomatoes, ketchup packets, dipping-sauce containers, and half-eaten baked potatoes and chicken tenders, but it was so much fun.

That was the only time Malik and I ever really hung out one-on-one outside of baseball.

I pick up the Wendy's wrapper and stuff it into my pocket.

BYE BYE BIRDIE

"That was some good ice cream," Mom says. "Whosever idea it was to go to A La Mode before the show, you're brilliant."

"Mom, you know it was your idea," Haley says.

"Then I guess I'm brilliant."

We're walking across the plaza to the entrance of the Playhouse. Haley, Mom, and Zoey are in front of me. Their arms are locked, and they're skipping like Dorothy, the Scarecrow, and the Tin Man heading down the yellow brick road on their way to see the wizard.

It's opening night, and it feels like an opening because even though it's still not completely dark, those Hollywood-premiere searchlights are sweeping across the sky. There's also music playing, and on the kiosks in the plaza, there are gigantic posters of the different cast members. And all along the sides of the plaza are kids from the high school—I recognize some of them—dressed like it's the 1950s because that's when *Bye Bye Birdie* takes place.

"I'm so glad I tasted your sea salt caramel before ordering," Mom says, glancing back at me. "That was an excellent call, Silas."

"That's because I'm brilliant, too," I say.

"Whatever." Haley turns and rolls her eyes at me. "Right, Zoey?"

Haley hasn't left Zoey's side the whole night, which is how it is whenever Haley's around Zoey. At dinner, she had to sit on Zoey's side of the booth, and then at A La Mode, she had to sit on the stool next to her at the counter. And when it came time to order ice cream, as soon as Zoey changed her order from chocolate chip cookie dough to birthday cake, so did Haley.

Mom stops in front of the kiosk with the poster of the person playing the role of Albert and takes a picture.

Then she walks around to the other side and takes a picture of the poster of the person playing Kim.

"You have no idea how much I need a night like tonight," Mom says.

"Tonight's all about self-care," Zoey says, double-dimple grinning because that's what Mom has said at least ten times already this evening.

"I almost feel like a person again," Mom says.

"Impossible," I say.

"I heard that, Silas." Mom points her phone at the poster of the person playing Rosie. "The three of you go stand over there," she says. "That's who I played when I was in *Bye Bye Birdie* in middle school."

"We know, Mom." Haley rolls her eyes again. "You've told us."

As many times as Mom has told us tonight is all about "self-care," she's told us she played Rosie in her middle school's production of *Bye Bye Birdie* even more.

Mom takes the photo and then spins around. She sings a couple lines from "Put On a Happy Face" as she dances over and group-hugs the three of us. "You have no idea how much I need this tonight."

I do have an idea, and I'm pretty sure Mom knows

I have an idea because it's impossible not to notice who isn't here tonight, Semaj and Dad. But what I don't know is what she needed most about tonight—time away from Semaj or time away from Dad.

We start walking toward the entrance.

"Are we seeing Grace now?" Haley asks.

"Not until after the show," Mom says.

"You don't want to see her now," Zoey says. "Grace is a wreck before the curtain goes up on opening night. Talk about someone who could probably use some self-care right now!"

Tonight's been all about self-care for Zoey, too. She hasn't said a single word about her robotics competition this weekend, and the fact that she hasn't tells me just how nervous she is. Tonight's been all about taking her mind off it, so I won't be the first to bring it up. But I will wish her luck before we go—

"Hey, Number Three."

I turn. Webb's walking toward us. He's wearing a sport jacket and tie, and I don't think I've ever seen him dressed up like that, not even at the end-of-the-season awards dinner. He's holding hands with a short-haired woman in a yellow dress, and I know it's his wife because I've seen her in photos on Instagram, but I've never met her in person.

"Hi, Webb," I say. "What are you doing here?" I realize how stupid the question is the second I say it.

"Same thing you're doing here," he says, motioning to the marquee and then holding out his fist.

I give him a dap.

"This is my wife, Nina," he says, letting go of her hand. "Nina, this is Silas Wade, the Renegades star center fielder. And that's his mom, Erica, and his sister Haley, right?"

"That's me," Haley says, posing like she does at the end of a gymnastics routine.

"Nice to meet everyone." Nina waves.

"I'm Zoey." She raises her hand. "I've heard a lot about you, Webb."

I flinch, but no one notices because no one's looking at me. And even if they had noticed, only Zoey or Webb could've possibly known why. They're the ones who know about me—the *only* ones who know about me—and for the first time, they're in the same place at the same time.

Zoey knows that Webb knows, and Webb knows that Zoey knows, and they both know that Mom doesn't know.

I'm keeping score. I'm always keeping score because I'm always in this game. I can never not be in this game.

But it's not a game.

"Nice to meet you," Mom says, shaking Nina's hand. "How are you, Webb?"

"Hot!" he says, tugging on his collar. "Hottest day of the year, and she makes me wear this."

"We're at the theater on opening night." Nina gives him a look. "You can wear a jacket and tie for a change."

Webb holds up his hands and smiles. "What can I tell you?"

Does Nina know? Webb promised he wouldn't tell anyone, but does that apply to Nina? Dad tells Mom everything—or at least he used to tell Mom everything—so by telling Webb, did I also tell Nina?

"It's going to be a scorcher tomorrow," Webb says to me.

"Bring it on," I say. "Baseball weather."

"You know it! Perfect weather for a triple-header."

"You Renegades are going to cook out there tomorrow,"

Mom says. "I'm glad your first two games are in the morning." She taps her wrist and then locks arm with Haley again. "We need to find a bathroom before heading to our seats."

"And we still need to pick up our tickets." Webb motions to the will-call window. "It was good seeing everyone."

"Yes," Nina says. "Nice meeting everyone."

"See you bright and early." Webb holds up his hand.

I give him a high five.

"A high five!" Mom points and smiles. "Silas just did a big report on the baseball player who invented the high five. What was his name again?"

"Glenn Burke," I say.

"Did you tell Webb about it?"

"I did."

"Bright and early tomorrow morning, Number Three," Webb says as he and Nina head off. "Enjoy the show."

I breathe. I know Webb gave me that high five on purpose, and I know—

"Come here." Zoey grabs my arm and pulls me away from Mom and Haley. She's looking at me in a way I've

181

never seen her look at me before. "After tonight, we're no longer friends."

"What? Why not?"

"You know why."

I look to Mom and Haley, but Zoey grabs my chin and turns it back to her.

"I'm your girlfriend?" she says, squeezing my face. "What do you think we're doing every Wednesday when I go over there?" She imitates me. "Singing karaoke?"

I try to answer, but she's still gripping my face, and even if I could answer, I don't know what I'd say.

"I'm playing nice tonight, but I'm not doing it for you." She shoves my face away. "I'm doing it for Haley, Erica, and Grace." She points at me. "After tonight, I'm never talking to you again. I hate you, Silas Wade."

TRIPLE-HEADER DISASTER

I should be jumping out of my cleats walking to the plate to lead off our triple-header against the Knights, but instead, I'm in slow motion and have been ever since Zoey let go of my face in front of the Playhouse. I maybe slept an hour last night.

I peep the Knights pitcher. I was watching him during our team stretch before the game, but I don't remember anything about his motion, release point, velocity, or the type of pitches he throws.

I adjust my wristband, fix my helmet, and tug on

the bottom of my jersey. I rotate my bat, tap the plate on the corners, take three half swings, bounce the bat off my shoulder, and bring it about my head.

I'm going through the motions. Nothing about this feels natural.

"What say you, Number Three?" Webb claps from the third-base box. "Start us off."

The first pitch pops the catcher's mitt.

"That's a strike." The umpire raises his first.

I back out of the batter's box and look into our dugout. Malik's on deck, and Theo's in the hole. Ben-Ben, Luis, and Alexander are standing on the bench. Everyone else is against the fence.

Who knows? Who knew the other day? Who said something to someone? If someone said something to someone, everyone knows. *Everyone* knows.

I step back into the box, tap the plate a couple of times, bounce the bat off my shoulder, and bring it about my head.

"That one's a little low," the ump calls. "Ball one."

It's a good thing it was, because I didn't see the pitch until after it crossed the plate.

My bat feels heavy, and I know if my bat feels heavy, my timing's going to be off. I rest it on my shoulder and adjust my helmet. Then I wipe the corners of my eyes with my sweatband.

I'm not solar-powered today. I'm the opposite of solar-powered today.

"Renegades are ready, Renegades are ready," Webb says. "Show them how we do, Number Three."

The Knights pitcher rocks into his windup.

Bye Bye Birdie was incredible last night, but I only know it was incredible because everyone else said it was incredible. I spent the entire show thinking about Zoey and how—

I start to swing, but I don't want to swing, so I check my swing but not in time. I foul the chaser over our dugout.

"Incoming!" Malik's mom shouts and rings her cowbell. "Incoming!"

The ball lands nowhere close to the bleachers.

Malik's standing in the dugout with his arms covering his head.

His mom's not annoying too many people yet. Luis's

dad and Alexander's parents are the only other ones in our bleachers, which is how it usually is for the first few innings on triple-header days, especially when it's blazing like this. Mom and Dad aren't coming at all today because Dad has work and Mom couldn't find anyone to look after Semaj.

I wipe the sweat from around my eyes again. I never got to wish Zoey good luck because she told me she hated me and was never talking to me again before I got the chance.

"Strike three!" the umpire calls.

My bat doesn't move. It's the first time I've struck out looking all season.

"I got it! I got it! I got it!" Malik calls for the pop-up behind short. He drifts toward second and raises his glove to shield his eyes from the sun. "I got it!"

But from where I'm standing in center, I know Malik doesn't got it.

"Mine! Mine!" Ben-Ben shouts from second. His glove's also up, and he's moving to his right. "Mine! Mine!"

Malik stops and pulls back his glove.

Ben-Ben stops, too.

The ball falls between them. Carter charges off the mound and picks it up. By the time he does, the runner from second is crossing the plate, and the Knights are extending their lead to 4–0.

"Time-out, ump," Webb calls, walking out onto the field.

The ump raises his arms. "Time is called."

As he heads to the mound, Webb waves to Ben-Ben and Malik and then points to me. I'm still standing where I was when the ball left the bat. I want no part of what's about to go down at this meeting, but I can't show up Webb, so I jog in.

"Happy now?" Webb says. He takes the upside-down sunglasses off the brim of Ben-Ben's cap and then grabs the pair off Malik's. "We told you this would happen."

"My bad," Ben-Ben says. "My bad."

Malik takes out his mouthguard. "Yeah. Sorry, Webb," he says.

"Your bad? You're sorry?" Webb stuffs the sunglasses into his back pocket. "We can't keep giving away outs.

That's what we did in the opener, and that's why we lost." He puts his hands on his hips. "We're beating ourselves out here."

We lost the opener 5–1. The game had been tied 1–1 going into the sixth, but Jason airmailed a throw that led to a run, Ernesto missed a cutoff that led to another, and then their DH smacked a two-out, two-run single that put the game out of reach.

"Why didn't you call it?" Ben-Ben asks. "Why didn't you call it?"

It takes a second to realize he's talking to me.

"The play was right in front of you," he says. "Why didn't you call it?"

I didn't call it because I was thinking about Zoey and what she may have said when she found out what I'd said about her. I was thinking that if she said something to someone, then he, Malik, and Carter, and everyone on the Renegades might know about me.

That's why I went 0 for 4 with three strikeouts in the opener. That's why I'm 0 for 2 in this game.

"I thought . . . I thought Carter was going to call it."

"No way." Ben-Ben waves his hands. "No way."

"You always make that call," Malik says.

"Yeah, you always call it," Carter says.

"The play was right in front of you," I say.

I look at Webb. He's staring at me in a way I'm not used to.

"Shake it off, Malik," I say, patting his shoulder with my glove.

He shrugs it off.

I flinch. Everyone sees. *Everyone.*

"What's up with you today, Silas?" Ben-Ben asks.

I swallow. "Me?"

"Yeah, you," Ben-Ben says. "You haven't hit the ball past the pitcher all day."

I wave my glove at him. "Well, I'm not the one dropping pop-ups."

"Well, I'm not the one making up stories about imaginary girlfriends and—"

"Are you kidding me right now?" Webb cuts him off. "Gentlemen, I have no idea what this is, but whatever it is, you need to work it out. But not right now. Right now, you need to put whatever this is aside and play Renegades baseball. That's it. Renegades baseball now, work it out later. Full stop." He claps at each of us. "Come on now. Let's get this last out."

"Rock 'n' roll," Malik says.

"One more." Ben-Ben pats Carter's shoulder with his glove. "One more."

"Renegades are ready." Webb claps as he backpedals away. "Renegades are ready."

Ben-Ben knows. Ben-Ben knows because Zoey told him. They're in the same robotics club. I never realized they were. I can't believe I never realized they were.

I turn around and jog back out to center. I'm trying not to cry. I'm doing everything in my power not to cry.

I dip my gray hand towel into the melted ice at the bottom of the cooler and then drape it over my head. The cold water drips down my neck and rolls down my shoulders and back. The heat and humidity have sapped me of everything. The heat and humidity have sapped all the Renegades of everything.

We lost the second game 10–2. On Carter's first pitch after the dropped pop fly, he gave up a two-run homer.

Then the Knights scored four more in the next inning, three on a bases-loaded single and two-base throwing error.

We're all sitting in the shade behind the bleachers. Luis is next to me on the other side of the cooler. I have the towel over my head, and I'm staring at the apricot fruit bars in my cap on the grass.

"That ump was the worst," Carter says. "I'd throw a pitch, and he'd call it a ball. Then I'd throw the same pitch, and he'd call it a strike."

"The ump isn't why you gave up seven runs," Malik says.

"I gave up seven runs because you couldn't catch a pop-up," Carter says.

"No," Malik says. "That was one pop-up and one run."

"What are you talking about?" Carter says. "That was three runs. Two more scored on the next pitch."

"Dude, you threw the pitch!" Malik yells.

"You were the reason I threw the pitch," Carter says. "It should've been three outs."

I haven't said a word the whole time I've been sitting here because I'm still too stunned to speak. How did I miss that Ben-Ben and Zoey know each other? How did I miss they're in robotics together? How well do they know each other? What else have they said about me?

"That umpire was the worst," Kareem says.

"The next time he makes a bad call," Carter says, "I'm saying something."

"I know, right?" Kareem says. "I'm saying something, too."

"Shut up, Snickers," Theo says. "You're not saying anything."

"Snickers." Luis shakes his head.

I peek out from under my towel. Theo is spitting seeds at Kareem, and Luis is smirking, but I don't say anything. I should, but I don't.

Kareem reaches into his Renegades bag and takes out his beef jerky. He's pretending not to feel the sunflower seeds and hear the digs and see the looks, but he does. We all know he does.

I glance at Theo. He's sitting in the exact spot where I had all the costumes laid out on the grass the other day. If I hadn't done my show, Theo and Kareem would have never made the comments. If they'd never made those comments, Webb would've never heard about it and said something, and Coach Noles and Brayden would still be on the Renegades. If they were still on the Renegades, the rest of the Renegades would've never been talking about them in the bleachers, and I would've never said what I did about Zoey.

I rub my eye with my palm. If I'd never told Zoey, none of this would have happened. None of this.

We're going to lose the next game. The Renegades are about to get swept in a triple-header by a team that should have a hard time scoring runs against us, and I'm the reason. I know I'm the reason.

"We're not losing this next game," I blurt out. I yank the towel off my head and swat the grass. "The Renegades aren't losing three in a row to the Knights."

"If you keep striking out, we will," Ben-Ben says. "Try getting on base."

"I'm going to," I say. "Believe me."

"Believe you?" Ben-Ben says. "Whatever you say, dude."

I look right at Ben-Ben, but I don't say anything. I can't believe this is happening, I can't believe this is happening, I can't believe this is happening.

"What?" Ben-Ben says. "What are you looking at?"

I still don't say anything.

"Dude, the whole team knows you're a liar," he says.

I flinch. The whole team sees me flinch. What did Zoey say to Ben-Ben? How much did she say to Ben-Ben? They all know what she said, but I have no idea what she said, and even if I did know—

"Anyway, I have a girlfriend," Ben-Ben mocks me. He stands up and flips his hair. "I'm kicking it with that girl Zoey."

I press my trembling palms against the grass, and when I do, I realize it's not just my hands that are shaking. My whole body is.

"I'm at her house every Wednesday." Ben-Ben flips his hair again. "We're the only ones there." He stares down at me. "What do you think we're doing, singing karaoke?"

I peep Malik. He shakes his head and looks away.

"So what is it?" Ben-Ben kneels in front of me. "Is she your girlfriend or not?"

I don't answer because I can't answer, because all my strength is going toward holding myself up and fighting my tears.

"Liar." Ben-Ben stands back up and kicks the bottom of my cleat. "Dude, you and your *girlfriend* need to get your stories straight."

IT'S NOT OKAY!

"No!" I shout, throwing back my comforter. "Semaj, put it down!"

"Bat," she says.

"Put it down!"

"Baseball bat." She taps the end of my bed with my yellow Wiffle.

I was dead asleep until two seconds ago, and when I opened my eyes, I was greeted by the sight of Semaj in her onesie standing at the foot of my bed holding my bat like a lightsaber.

"You don't belong in here!" I kick off the rest of my covers.

"Semaj baseball bat," she says. "Semaj baseball bat."

"Put it down!" I jump out of bed.

"Semaj baseball—"

"No!" I grab the bat and rip it out of her hands. "Put it down!"

"Silas!" Mom bursts into my room.

"Get her out of here!" I shake the bat in Semaj's face.

"Silas!" Mom grabs my arm.

"She was about to smash my José Altuve!"

"She wasn't near your bobbleheads!"

"Yes, she was!" I whirl around and fling the bat onto my bed. It bounces off the wall and lands on the floor by the closet.

"Silas!" Mom shouts again.

Semaj starts to cry.

"What is she doing in my room?" I yell.

"This is how I have to start my Sunday morning?" Mom wraps her arms around Semaj and glares at me. "You happy now?"

"No, I'm not happy now!"

Mom squeezes and rocks Semaj. "It's okay," she says. "It's okay, Pumpkin, shh." She shakes her head at me.

I shake my head back. I'm wide awake now, and right away, I think about yesterday. I think about standing in center field during the last inning of the third game—a game we lost 5–0—with tears streaming down my cheeks.

I have no idea when I finally fell asleep last night, because I couldn't stop thinking about how Zoey and Ben-Ben know each other from robotics. I missed it. It never crossed my mind. But it has to cross my mind. I can't miss things like that anymore, because if I do miss things like that, people are going to find out about me. And people *can't* find out about me.

I press my palms against my temples. I should have never listened to the kids in the videos, and I should have never listened to what was written in the letters, and I should have never said something to Zoey, and I should have never said something to Webb, and I should have never—

"Silas, I need your help around here," Mom says, speaking softer. She's still rocking Semaj, who's still crying. "I can't do this by myself."

"She came into my room and woke me up," I say.

"I know she did, but I need you to be more sensitive to—"

"I need to be more sensitive?" I point to myself. "I'm always sensitive. I have no choice but to be sensitive—"

"Lower your voice." Mom cuts me off. "Please don't upset Semaj even more than—"

"No! I don't want to lower my voice. I'm tired of lowering my voice." I flail my arms. "I'm tired of being sensitive. People need to be sensitive of me. People need to be—"

"Hey, hey, hey." Dad walks in with his hands up. "What's going on?"

"Silas is having a rough morning," Mom answers calmly.

"Is this about baseball yesterday?" Dad asks.

"Baseball bat," Semaj says, whimpering.

"It's okay." Mom pulls her closer. "Shh."

"Losing three games like that can be tough." Dad rubs his bald spot. "You're having such a great season and then to drop—"

"This isn't about baseball, Dad." I flail my arms again.

"Okay, then what's this about, Swade? What seems—"

"That!" I shout. "That's what this is about!"

"What?" Dad's hands are back up.

"Stop calling me that!" I stomp my foot. "I don't want you calling me Swade anymore!"

"Then I won't call you Swade anymore." He nods once. "Okay?"

"No! It's not okay. You say it is, but it's not." I smack my sides. "How can you be so clueless?"

"Silas, this isn't like you," he says. "I don't know where this is coming—"

"I know you don't! That's the problem."

"Silas, lower your voice." Mom strokes Semaj's hair. "Please."

"You're so clueless, Dad! Do you ever hear anyone else call me Swade anymore? Do you? Don't you see the looks I give you when you do? Don't you see the looks Mom gives you? She knows how much I hate it. Ask her. Oh, wait, you can't ask her, because you two don't even talk to each other anymore."

"Silas, please," Mom says.

"No, Mom," I say. "It's the truth, and you know it. Stop pretending it's not." I smack my sides again and turn back to Dad. "I'm glad you can't come to my games anymore. Do you know why? Because it's humiliating. It's humiliating when you call me Swade in front of everyone. I'm not Swade! I don't want kids calling me that. I'm not Swade!"

"Okay." Dad leans against the doorframe. "I've retired the nickname."

I sit down on the edge of my bed and cover my eyes with my palms. I think about the text I sent Zoey last night when I couldn't sleep. I wished her luck in the rest of the competition, but before pressing Send, I stared at the screen for the longest time because I would need to know if she read it. And I needed her to read it, and I still don't know if she has because I'm afraid to check and see.

I slide my hands around my head and press them against my temples again. Why did I tell Zoey? Why did I tell Webb? How could I do this to myself? How could I have not known this would happen?

"I don't want to play baseball anymore," I say.

"Baseball," Semaj says.

"Why not?" Mom asks, still speaking calmly.

"Wow," Dad says. "I didn't see that coming."

"Gil, please," Mom says. "Let him answer. Why not, Silas?"

"I just don't." I lower my hands and shake my head. "I'm not . . . I'm not having fun anymore."

"Does this have something to do with your coach leaving the team last—?"

"No, Dad, it doesn't," I interrupt. "I'm just not having fun anymore. I haven't for a while."

"Why is this the first we're hearing about it?"

"Gil, please," Mom says again.

"Can I skip practice on Tuesday?" I ask her.

"Tuesday or the rest of the season?" she asks.

"Tuesday," I say. "I need a self-care day."

Mom smiles. "I can go along with that," she says. "Gil?"

Dad shrugs. "If Silas is missing practice," he says, "he needs to be the one to tell his coach, not you."

"I know," I say. "It's a team rule. Webb says you have to call if you can't make a practice or a game."

I put off making the call until after dinner. Since my phone is in my room, I use Mom's to call Webb. I dial his number, press Speaker, and place the phone on the kitchen island. I want the call to go right to voice mail—I need the call to go right to voice mail—but it doesn't. Now I need him not to answer. He doesn't after the first ring, he doesn't after the second, he doesn't after the third . . .

"Erica Wade," Webb answers. "How are you this evening?"

"Hi . . . hi, Webb," I say, swiveling my stool. "It's me, Silas."

"Hey there, Silas."

"You're on . . . you're on speaker," I say. "I'm here with my mom."

"Hello, Webb," Mom says. She folds her arms.

"How's everyone this evening?" Webb asks.

"Good." I swallow. "Listen, um, I'm not able to make it to practice on Tuesday, and I'm calling—"

"Is everything okay?"

"Yeah, yeah. I'm just calling because I can't make it, and . . . and I know we have to call when we can't make it."

"I appreciate it," Webb says. "Am I going to see you Thursday, Silas?"

"Oh, yeah, yeah," I say. "I'll be there Thursday."

"Then I'll see you Thursday."

"Thanks, Webb."

"High five, Silas."

27

FACE-TO-FACE

"Waiting for your partner in crime?" Ms. Washington asks.

"Something like that," I say.

I'm standing by the door to Ms. Washington's room, looking down the long hallway toward the cafeteria. I got here early because I still haven't seen Zoey, and I need to. She's avoiding me, and she knows I'm probably waiting for her, which is why she still isn't here. But she is coming because she's finished with robotics, so she's going to have to see me.

"How was the show?" Ms. Washington asks.

"Good," I say without turning to her. "Really good."

"That's what I hear," Ms. Washington says. "I can't wait to see it on Friday."

I still don't know how Zoey did in the competition because I purposely haven't asked anyone, and I wore my buds during the morning announcements in case they said something. I want Zoey to be the one to tell me, and I want her to know that I wanted her to be the one.

"Move."

Zoey brushes me with her bag and dips into the classroom. She came from the other direction.

I follow her in. "Hey, how did robotics go?"

She doesn't answer or slow down.

"Did you guys win?"

She stops. "What do you want, Silas?"

"I want to know . . . I'm asking you how you did. I honestly don't know if you won—"

"Did you think I was joking the other night?" She raises her voice.

Other kids are walking in and watching.

"Is this a skit?" Ms. Washington slides closer. "Is this something you two practiced over—"

"I told you I hated you and never wanted to talk to you again," Zoey says, loudly. "Which word in that sentence do you not understand?"

"Oh, this is real." Ms. Washington covers her mouth. "Zoey, I—"

"We won!" Zoey shouts. "My team won. You happy now, Silas? Is that what you *needed* to know? Fine, now you know. Now get out of my life!"

28

GLENN BURKE AFTER

When Glenn Burke died, the man who invented the high five could barely lift his hand. That's what it says in so many of the articles I read about him, including the one on my laptop right now.

I'm in the kitchen on the stool at the end of the island. Up until this afternoon, the only place I've ever read about Glenn Burke is in my bedroom or in the bathroom. I'm reading about Glenn Burke out here because I have the apartment to myself all afternoon. It's completely quiet. All I hear is the hum of the refrigerator and the creaking of the stool when I shift or swivel. I can't remember the last time the apartment was this quiet during the day.

When Glenn Burke played for the Pendulum Pirates in the San Francisco Gay Softball League, he was voted Player of the Year, and when he played in the Gay Olympics, his team won the World Series. But the reason Glenn played for those teams was because he couldn't play Major League Baseball, because Major League Baseball didn't want him. He couldn't play the sport he loved because of who he was.

I check my phone on the stool. I can still see the conversation with Dad from earlier. He wanted to know if he should come home to check on me, and I told him he didn't have to. Then he asked me if I was sure, and I told him I was positive, at which point he sent me his double emoji.

At practice right now, I'd be doing infield work, taking ground balls with Malik and Luis and Ben-Ben and Jason. Webb would be telling us to get low.

"Pretend you're sitting on the toilet," he'd say. "Squat down lower. Pretend you're pooping in the woods! Lower!"

We'd all be cracking up.

I press my palms against my temples. Forced out of baseball, Glenn Burke started drinking and doing drugs. One night, crossing the street, he got hit by a car and broke his leg in three places. He couldn't hold down a job, and before long, he was homeless. Then he started committing crimes. Then he went to jail.

Glenn Burke was forty-two when he died in 1995. That's how old Dad is. Glenn Burke died of AIDS. That's what happened to most people when they got AIDS back then. I learned all about it on YouTube. I had no idea that's what it was like back then, and I'm pretty sure most kids have no idea that's what it was like. I've been checking out some movie trailers because I want to know more and saw one for this documentary called *How to Survive a Plague*, but I'm not sure I'm ready for it.

I look at the bright orange sticky notes on the counter under my spoon. The one with CHECK THE FREEZER was on my pillow when I got home from school. The one with SELF-CARE and the smiley faces was stuck to the front of the sealed pint of sea salt caramel in the freezer. The sea salt caramel pint is no longer sealed or in the freezer—it's empty at the bottom of the garbage can under the sink.

I click a tab and go back to the page with the coming-out video of the kid with the spiky bleached-blond hair and the row of rainbow bracelets on both wrists. It's the video I keep watching over and over and over, and it's paused at the point right before he starts talking about how he told one of his friends he was gay, and that friend told someone, and now he thinks everyone knows.

29

JUMP & GRIND

"Welcome to the Jump & Grind," I say, tapping the guest check pad with the cap end of the blue ballpoint. "Can I take your order?"

The woman standing on the other side of the counter smiles at Mom, who's wiping down the area around the pitchers of ice water at the table in the corner.

"I'll have a large iced latte with almond milk and an extra shot," the woman says.

"Write that down." Kaila nudges me. "You'll never remember."

"I'll remember." I touch my temple.

"You're gonna mess up your orders that way," Kaila says. "Write it down."

"Yes, boss," I say.

During last-period math, I texted Mom to see if she needed help after school, and when she asked why I wasn't doing karaoke with Zoey like I usually do on Wednesday, I didn't give her a reason. I just told her we weren't. So Mom picked me up—which was exactly what I wanted—and now this afternoon, Kaila is teaching me to work the counter. And since she still can't grip a pen because of the stitches in her hand, I'm really working.

"You gotta be quicker with the customers," Kaila says, punching the order into the tablet. "People don't wanna wait in line all day."

"There's no one else on line." I motion to the woman across the counter. "She's the only one here."

"It ain't always gonna be like this." Kaila rips the guest check off the pad and hands it back to the barista by the espresso machine. "Your order will be right up," she says to the woman.

I tap Kaila's good hand with the ballpoint and

motion to Mom, who's moved on to straightening the stirrers and straws at the self-service station.

"You should see her with the bobbleheads in my room," I say.

"What's that mean?"

"It means, that's how she is at home. Everything has to be perfect."

"It's dope she's like that," Kaila says. "Look at this place."

"I guess, but—"

"What do you mean, *you guess*?" She grabs the top of my head with her good hand. "Look around, man. This place is beautiful." She rotates my head back and forth. "Really look around. Take in the details."

I look at the black-and-white photographs of Nina Simone, Sarah Vaughan, Billie Holiday, and Ella Fitzgerald on the wall above the circular booths. I look at the Little Free Library stocked with picture books and shelved alphabetically by the illustrators' last names. I look at the two long tables in the middle with the bowling alley tops. I look at the blue-and-yellow equal sign sticker on the window by the door right below the Jump & Grind sign.

"It is kinda dope," I say.

"Kinda?" Kaila says, tucking her hair back into her Jump & Grind snapback. "This place is inspired. Erica wants everyone to feel welcome here and really means it. I love working here 'cause . . . 'cause it don't feel like work. She gets people."

She does. Mom gets me, which is why she didn't press me for the reason I wasn't doing karaoke. If she had, it would've become a thing, and neither of us wanted a thing this afternoon.

"See the guy on the sofa over there?" Kaila says, pointing.

"Yeah."

"He's having a party here Saturday night for his mom," Kaila says. "She's retiring. She's been an elementary school teacher for, like, thirty years or something, and when Erica found out, she told the guy he should have the party here. He didn't ask. She just offered. Erica's a boss."

"No wonder she likes you so much," I say, flipping my hair and grinning. "You're like the president of her fan club."

"No, she's a boss," Kaila says. "The real deal. What

you see is what you get." She raises her arms. "And that's me. What you see is what you get. Authentic."

Authentic.

It takes me a second to remember where I heard that word before. Webb said it to me the other day when we were having our catch.

Authentic.

30

MALIK

"Switch, Renegades," Jason says, leading the prepractice stretch. "Last one."

I start to get up, but Coach Rockford holds out his hand.

"Not you," he says. "No need for me to get down there. You get a double session."

Coach Rockford's my stretch partner today because Malik's not here yet. We're all in front of the first-base dugout, and we're up to hamstrings, which, like always, is our last stretch before we run.

Mom dropped me off just as practice was starting, which was exactly how I planned it. If I'd been early like when Grace brings me, I would've had to sit with everyone and deal with everyone. I know I'm going to have to—and I will—but I couldn't the second I got here.

"Other leg," Jason says.

I lower my right leg and raise my left. Coach Rockford bends down and leans forward so I can rest it on his shoulder. As he inches toward me and pushes my leg back to me, I feel the stretch, close my eyes, and keep score. Ben-Ben hasn't looked my way. Luis nodded to me when I got here and kinda sorta smiled when we made eye contact during jumping jacks. Alexander usually stretches with Ernesto, and Theo usually stretches with Kareem, but today they switched partners. Kareem waved when he saw me getting out of the car, and he gave me a dap during shoulder stretches. The other three ignored me.

"Okay, gentlemen," Webb says, clapping. "Let's do this. Three laps today. Three laps and then we meet at home plate. Let's go."

We all bounce to our feet and take off, and by the time we're running along the warning track in front of the outfield fence, Luis, Ben-Ben, and I are in front.

"I wonder where Malik is," I say.

Neither answers, not that I expected Ben-Ben to.

"I hope he gets—"

"Dude, he's not coming," Luis interrupts me.

"Why not?" I ask.

"If you'd been here Tuesday, you'd know," Ben-Ben snaps. "You'd know."

"Know what?" I say.

"Malik's off the Renegades," Luis says. "His parents pulled him off the team."

I stop. All the Renegades pass me. I put my hands on my knees and bend over. I'm going to be sick, and there's nothing I can do about it. I clasp my hands behind my head and stand back up enough to see my teammates running down the third-base line. I'm still in the outfield.

I start to slow-jog, and when I reach the left-field line, I keep going straight and run until I reach the batting cages. I bend over again and start to retch. This time when I try to stand back up to catch my breath, I lose my lunch.

31

MAKING THE CALL

"Don't pick up, don't pick up, don't pick up," I say after I press the Call button.

I'm outside our apartment building, standing against the railing by the steps. Everyone's inside—Dad's giving Semaj a bath, Mom's still on her call with the caterer for tomorrow night's retirement party, and Haley's dancing around her room with her headphones on. That's why I was able to dip out without anyone noticing.

"Number Three." Webb picks up on the first ring. "What say you?"

"Hey, Webb." I swallow. "Listen, I—"

"How are you feeling? Any better?"

Webb knows I wasn't feeling well at practice yesterday, but he doesn't know I got sick. No one does. By the time Coach Rockford came to check on me by the batting cages, I was already heading back to the field.

"A little better," I say. "I'm still—"

"Everything okay, Silas?" Webb asks. "You need to talk?"

"No," I say. "No, I'm good."

"You sure?"

"Yeah, I just . . . um . . . I can't make it to the game."

"Really?" Webb says. "Ouch."

"Yeah, I know. I'm sorry."

"Silas, did something happen yesterday?"

"No."

"Are you sure?"

"No . . . I mean . . . I mean, yes. Yes, I'm sure. Nothing happened. I just can't make it."

"This is really last-minute, Silas. It leaves us with only nine players for tomorrow."

"Yeah, I know . . . I just . . . I can't make it, Webb."

"We always like to have at least ten. I hope there's

still time for us to get a replacement call-up from one of the select teams. The Renegades are—" Webb stops.

I check the phone to see if we're still connected. We are.

"Silas, you sure you're okay?" he asks.

I swallow.

"Silas?"

"Thanks."

32

DEALING WITH DAD

I'm sitting at the kitchen table with a glass of chocolate milk and one of the blueberry muffins Mom brought home yesterday. Dad just turned off the TV in the bedroom, which means he's finished getting dressed, and he'll be in here in three, two, one . . .

"Good morning, Silas." He stops in the doorway. "What . . . what's going on? Where's your uniform?"

I'm still wearing the navy sweats and gray tank undershirt I wore to bed.

"Why aren't you dressed?"

I was able to avoid this conversation last night, but I knew it was coming first thing this morning.

"I'm not playing today," I say.

"What are you talking about? You have two games. Go get dressed."

"I don't feel like it."

"You don't feel like it?" Dad rubs his bald spot. "What do you mean you don't feel like it?"

"I mean, I don't. I don't want to go."

"I thought you said the team was down players because one of the coaches—"

"I already called Webb." I cut him off. "They'll call a kid up from—"

"When did you call?"

I swallow. "Last night."

"Last night?" Dad steps to the table and grips the back of a chair. "You knew about this last night and didn't say anything?"

I pick up the muffin and break it in half.

"You intentionally waited for your mother to leave this morning so you wouldn't have to tell her, didn't you?"

It's more a statement than a question. I don't respond.

"You know she's not going to be home until late tonight," he says.

I put the top of the muffin next to my milk and the stump back on the plate.

"I need to think." Dad looks at the clock on the microwave. "I was going to go to your game for a few innings and then head into the office and get that over with, but now . . ." He bangs the chair with the heels of his hands. "I'd have scheduled my day so differently if I'd known about this."

"You still can," I say.

"No, I can't, Silas!" he snaps. "Your mother left already, remember?"

"Sorry," I say.

"Yeah. Me too."

I really am sorry that I didn't think about what my not saying anything last night would do to his day or Mom's day or anyone else's day.

"Sorry," I say again.

"I'm worried about you." He softens his tone.

"I'm fine, Dad."

"I hope so."

"I am."

He pulls out the chair and sits. "Well, if you're not fine . . ." He puts an elbow on the table and his chin in his hand. "If you're not fine, I know you're not going to say anything to me, but I hope you would say something to your mother. If you're in some kind of—"

"Thanks." I don't let him finish.

He points to the muffin stump on my plate.

"All yours," I say.

"I love you, Silas."

33

BROKEN PEOPLE

"Wake up," Haley says.

I open my eyes. Haley's standing over me wearing her purple-and-black gymnastics warm-ups and her headphones around her neck.

"Wake up, Silas." She shakes my pillow. "Your—"

"What are you doing?" I push her away. "Get out of—"

"Your coach from the other night is here." She heads for my door.

"What?"

"Your baseball coach is in the kitchen with Mommy and Daddy," she says, walking out.

I sit up and blink hard. Webb's here? Why is Webb here? How long has he been here? Did he come on his own? Did Mom and Dad invite him? What has he said to them? What does Mom know about yesterday? Did Dad talk to her when she got home?

I slide my feet into my flip-flops and rub my eyes with my palms. I still have on the same navy sweats and gray tank I wore all day yesterday, the same sweats and tank I wore to bed the night before last. I haven't been outside since I got home from school on Friday.

I check myself in the mirror on my closet and then head for the door, but I stop because along the bottom frame of my bulletin board is a new row of stickers. Haley must've put them there just now. Each sticker has a draw-ing of hands high-fiving. There are also high-five stickers held up by the same pushpin as my baseball schedule.

I let out a long breath. Haley has no idea how much seeing these stickers right now means to me. She has no idea how much I *needed* to see these stickers right now.

"What say you, Number Three?" Webb raises his black-and-white Jump & Grind coffee mug when I walk into the kitchen.

"Hi, Webb." I half wave.

He's standing at the island in the spot where I called him to say I wouldn't be at practice the other day. Mom's on a stool next to him with her hands around her mug. Dad's at the kitchen table.

"Hi, Mom," I say softly. "Hi, Dad."

Dad doesn't look up from his tablet. Mom says nothing.

"We split the twin bill yesterday," Webb says. "Lost the opener but came back to win the nightcap."

"Good," I say.

"Then again, the Cyclones gave us that second game," Webb adds, smiling. "They found ways to lose I didn't even know existed." He puts down the mug. "But a win's a win, right?"

"A win's a win," I say.

"The kid we called up from the select team, Cole Lenk, was quite the ballplayer. He had a couple of hits and threw a runner out trying to go first to third from right."

"Nice," I say.

Webb raps the edge of the island. "Mr. and Mrs.

Wade," he says, "would you mind if Silas and I step outside for a few minutes?"

"Did you tell them?" I ask.

We're on the steps outside my building. I ask the question the second we sit down.

"No, I didn't tell them," he says. "You know I didn't."

"I know, but—"

"I would never do that to you, Silas."

I know he wouldn't, but I asked anyway because I had to ask anyway.

"I did tell them you told an untruth about your friend Zoey," he says. "And I told them that your teammates called you on it and that you deserved it."

"Yeah."

He takes a sip of coffee and puts the mug down on the step. "The third baseman on my college team was gay. Colby Brooks." He tucks his hands into the pouch pocket of his hoodie. "Started at third base my junior and senior year. No one cared that he was gay—not the players, not the coaches, not the fans." He bumps my shoulder. "Not that we had many fans."

I bump him back.

"He was there to play ball, and that's exactly what he did. He was everything you could ask for in a teammate. That's what mattered."

"It didn't for Glenn Burke," I say.

"No, it didn't," Webb says. "You're right. Baseball wasn't ready for an openly gay baseball player back then. It would've been unthinkable at the time."

"Glenn Burke was an anachronism," I say.

"I guess you can say he was." Webb smiles. "Except you can't say he didn't belong."

"Glenn Burke belonged."

"The game's come a long way since back then. It still has a ways to go, but it's come a long way." He bumps my shoulder again. "It's not unthinkable that someone like you could play. You're no anachronism, buddy."

The door to the building opens, and Ms. Perkins and Rex charge out.

"Someone has to go!" she says as Rex pulls her down the walk.

Webb grabs his mug and jumps up. I slide across the step.

"Sorry, sorry, sorry," she says as they hurry past. "Thank you, Silas. Thank you, Silas's friend."

At the end of the walk, Rex heads for the tree with the sign like he always does.

"Who's walking who?" Webb says softly.

"It's like that all the time," I say.

Webb jumps down the stairs and pours what's left of his coffee onto the grass. Then he puts his mug in the middle of the walk in front of the bottom step and sits back down.

"Let's see if you still got game," he says, pulling a bag of ranch-flavored sunflower seeds out of his pouch pocket.

"Ranch?" I say. "You said you only eat original." I stand up and start imitating him. "Sunflower seeds have one flavor and one flavor only," I say. "Original. You'll never catch me eating cracked pepper or dill pickle or smokehouse BBQ or nacho—"

"Sit your butt down, Number Three." He grabs my tank and pulls me back to the step. "So I did my homework before coming here this morning," he says, opening the bag of seeds. "I prepared for this conversation because . . . well, this isn't necessarily my area of expertise, and I wanted to be sure I was doing right by you."

"Okay," I say.

"Silas, what happened to Glenn Burke is not going to happen to you." He pops a handful of seeds into his mouth and stuffs them into his cheek. "Things have changed since back then, things are changing right now, and things will continue to change."

"Not everywhere," I say.

"No, not everywhere. You're right. But they'll continue to change because of people like you." He spits a seed at the coffee mug. It lands a few inches in front of it. "I wish I could look you in the eye right now and tell you things are changing everywhere, but I'd be lying." He points his finger back and forth. "When we talk about this, I'm going to tell it like it is." He spits another seed. This one hits the base of the mug. "Getting closer."

I reach into the bag, toss a handful into my mouth, and tuck them in my cheek. Then I spit one at the mug. It lands on the bottom step.

"Here's telling it like it is," Webb says. "You be you, Silas. No matter what anyone tells you, no matter what anyone says, your existence—who you are—is not controversial."

Webb stands up and spits a seed that lands in the mug.

"Pow!" he says, imitating me. "Pow, pow!" He flips his hair.

"You still got it."

"Still got it?" he says. "I never lost it!"

I roll my tongue around the inside of my cheek for a seed and spit it at the mug. It glances off the handle.

"Getting closer," I say, smiling.

Webb sits back down. "Your coming out . . . your coming out is going to be extraordinary, Silas. It's not going to be easy, but it will be extraordinary. And it's a process. You already know that. It's not something that's going to happen over the course of a few days or weeks or months. It's going to be exciting and embarrassing and frustrating and hilarious and tragic and empowering, and . . . it's going to be a lot like life." He grips the back of my neck. "You're going to meet so many people on this journey, Silas. People who will love you and celebrate you, and the impact you're going to have on them will be extraordinary." He squeezes. "That's happening already. You've impacted me."

"It didn't impact Malik," I say.

He sighs and lets go of my neck. "Malik."

"Do you know why he left the team?" I ask.

"It wasn't Malik's decision, buddy."

I spit a seed that sails over the mug. Then I spit another that hits the handle again.

Webb spits a seed that bounces off the lip. "Oh!" he says. "That was almost two for me and none for you."

"Almost."

"Here's some more telling it like it is," Webb says. "You can't fix broken people."

"What do you mean, broken?"

"Ms. Anderson, my AP lit teacher in high school, used to say that to us all the time. You can't fix broken people. She said it's one of the most difficult lessons kids have to learn. For some, it's a hard truth they never come to terms with."

"Broken?"

"Yeah, we can all use some work and repairs," Webb says, nodding. "Some of us more than others, some of us a lot more than others. But it's up to the individual. It's always up to the individual. You can offer help and support, but you can't do the fixing."

"You can't fix broken people," I say.

"No," Webb says. "And on your journey, unfortunately, you're going to meet a lot of these broken people who are going to have a hard time with who you are."

I think about Glenn Burke and all the broken people he had to face, all the broken people he couldn't fix. I think about Al Campanis, the Dodgers vice president, who wanted him to get married. I think about Tommy Lasorda, the Dodgers manager, who wanted him away from the organization and out of his life. I think about Billy Martin, the A's manager, who made sure everyone knew that people like Glenn Burke didn't belong in baseball.

Then it hits me. The other day in center field, when Webb and I had our catch, Webb said, *You can't fix broken people*. I knew I'd heard that before.

"What happened with Coach Noles?" I ask.

Webb sighs again. "Coach Noles . . . Coach Noles sees the world differently than I do, and I'm not willing to agree to disagree with him." Webb looks at me. "Silas, you deserve to be more than tolerated. You deserve to be accepted. You deserve to be loved for exactly who you are. Full stop."

"Me be me," I say.

"Yes," Webb says. "You be you."

I spit a high-arcing seed that lands in the mug. "Pow!" I jump up.

"It's about time." He holds up his hand.

I give him a high five and then spit another high-arcing seed that lands in the mug. "Oh!" I raise both fists. "Two for two!" I lean into Webb and flip my hair. "Pow! Pow!"

He pushes me away and stands up. "The Renegades are going through a rough patch," he says. "As a team and as individuals."

"I feel bad for Kareem," I say. "That nickname is going to stick."

"It sure is." He reaches back down for the bag of seeds and stuffs it into his hoodie. "Snickers is a keeper."

"I knew it the second Theo and Luis said it," I say. "But I'm not . . . I'm not going to call him it." I breathe. "Do any of the Renegades know?"

He leans against the railing. "Did you tell them?"

I shake my head.

"Then they don't know. They think you're a bragger and a liar, and they have every right to, but they don't know."

"Yeah." I spit the rest of my seeds into my hand and toss them onto the grass.

"I'm hoping we're able to weather these storms in time for the playoffs," Webb says. "Having you back . . . you are coming back, right?"

I breathe again. "I'm dreading it . . . I have to face everyone."

"That you do. You made up a lie and got busted for it. You need to own that."

"I made up two lies." I lean against the other railing. "The one about Zoey and the one about me."

"No," Webb says firmly. He holds up a finger. "One lie. What you said about your friend was an untruth, but that's it. Who you are is not a lie."

Webb spits a seed across the steps at me. It lands on my sweats, and I brush it off. I still have one more seed left in my mouth, and I think about spitting it at Webb. Instead, I tuck it into my cheek with my tongue.

"The Renegades want you back," Webb says. "They're not going to hold this against you."

"I don't know."

"I do. Don't underestimate your teammates, Silas. That's the same thing I said to you about your parents.

Don't underestimate the Renegades; don't underestimate Gil and Erica." Webb walks across to me. "You're an incredibly lucky kid. You might not think you are, but you are." He grips the back of my neck again. "Those two people in the kitchen right now love you very much. Not every kid in your position is so fortunate. Not even close."

"I know."

"They have your back, Silas. You're going to be okay."

"I know," I say.

"I know you do, but you need to hear it. You're going to be okay, buddy."

"Thanks," I say. I start to smile. "There's another reason I have to come back to the Renegades."

"Have to? Why's that?"

I hold up a finger and tongue the seed out of my cheek. Then I size up the mug and launch one more high-arcing shot. It lands in the center of the mug.

"Pow!" I hold up both hands.

Webb double-high-fives me. "Pow!"

We clasp hands.

"I have to come back to the Renegades because Glenn Burke never got the high five he deserves," I say. "I need to do something about that."

34

HALF WAVE

I'm sitting in Ms. Washington's waiting for class to start, and when Zoey walks in, I brace myself for her evil death stare. But instead, when she sees me looking, she moves her arm like she's about to wave but stops herself before she does. Then she heads for the other side of the room and sits down on the denim sofa between Daphne and Kaitlyn.

I go back to filling in the seams of the baseball I'm doodling on the cover of my spiral. Maybe it wasn't the start of a wave. Maybe I've just gotten so used to Zoey's death stare that anything other than her death stare looks friendly. Maybe she just was adjusting her books or rolling her shoulder.

I face Ms. Washington, standing in front of the whiteboard, and when she sees me look her way, she glances at Zoey and then crosses her hands over her chest, hunches her shoulders, and smiles.

She saw what I saw. Then again, it's Ms. Washington. Maybe she's just being dramatic.

35

HITTING RETURN

Dad reaches across the front seat and squeezes my shoulder. "I'll stick around as long as you want," he says.

I look out the window toward the field: Alexander and Ernesto are walking up the path toward the bleachers behind the first-base dugout; Luis, Carter, and Theo are soft-tossing on the infield; everyone else is getting ready by the backstop. I need to get out of the car and head over, and I will get out of the car and head over, but we've been sitting here for almost two minutes, and I still can't get myself to pull the handle and open the door.

"You don't have to stick around," I say, still looking out the window. "I'll be fine."

"I know I don't have to, but—"

"I'll be fine." I face him and take a breath. "Really."

"Then I'll see you here after practice, Silas."

"Thanks, Dad."

I open the door.

"What up, Silas?" Ben-Ben sees me first and bounces over. "What's up?"

"Hi, Ben-Ben," I say.

"We're stretch partners today." He holds out his fist.

I give him a dap. "Oh, cool."

I stare at Ben-Ben. I know Webb said something to the team, because there's no way Ben-Ben comes up to me like this on his own. But I'm okay that Webb said something, because I know whatever he said was what I wanted him to say, even without my knowing what he said.

"Luis is leading," Ben-Ben says, thumbing the field. "That's why we're stuck with each other."

I swallow. "Yeah."

"Nah, kidding." He shapes the brim of his cap and smiles. "We're good, dude."

"I'm sorry, Ben-Ben," I say. "I don't know why I said those things. I'm sorry . . . sorry for lying."

It's true. I don't know why I said those things about Zoey. I know part of the reason, but not the full reason. And no matter what the reason is, it's not enough of a reason, because you don't lie like that about your best friend. You never lie like that about your best friend.

"Hey, Silas." Kareem walks up.

"Hi, Kareem." I hold out my fist.

He gives me a dap and smiles. "I'm glad you came back," he says.

"I'm sorry, Kareem," I say. "I lied about Zoey. I don't know why I did, but I did. I'm sorry."

"I'm glad you came back," he says again.

I glance at Theo by the backstop. "Kareem, I'm sorry if I ever . . . I'm sorry if I wasn't always cool to you. I don't know why—"

"You're always cool to me, Silas," he says.

"Hey, man." Jason runs up and pats my chest with his glove. "Good to have you back. We need you."

"Sorry for telling those lies," I say, but Jason's already

running back onto the field. "Sorry for saying those things about Zoey. I don't know . . ."

Jason raises his glove without turning around.

"For-ev-er," Luis says, grinning as he walks up. "For-ev-er, for-ev-er."

He's imitating Squints from the scene in *The Sandlot* when he's telling the Legend of the Beast story.

We tap gloves.

"I'm leading the stretch," Luis says. "Ben-Ben's your partner today."

"Yeah, he told me."

"Hey!" Luis shouts to Ben-Ben. "Does he know?"

Ben-Ben gives him a look. "Know what?"

"Know what?" I ask Luis.

Luis waves his glove. "You'll know soon enough."

I swallow. "Is it bad?"

"Savage!" Luis laughs. "It's awesome."

"I'm sorry, Luis." I tap his chest with my glove. "I don't know why I lied about Zoey like that. I hate that I did. I'm sorry."

MOM AND SILAS TIME

I'm sitting at the long table with the bowling alley top in the middle of the Jump & Grind waiting for Mom and Kaila. They've been going over the schedule and work orders since closing a half hour ago. I already finished wiping down the tables, sweeping the floor, taking out the trash and recycling, restocking the self-serve station, and boxing up the leftover muffins and scones to take home for breakfast.

I worked the register like I did last Wednesday, but this week, I worked it on my own because Kaila's stitches are out and she's back to preparing beverages and making paninis and wraps.

"Thanks for everything," Kaila says, hugging Mom.

"No, Kaila, thank you," Mom says. "You have no idea how relieved I am this is working out."

"It's working out for me, too," she says. "See ya tomorrow, Erica." Kaila heads for the door but stops at my table. "I had fun today, Silas," she says.

"I know you did." I flip my hair. "You got to hang with me."

"Do you hear him?" She looks back at Mom.

"I ignore him when he gets like that." Mom points at me. "I'll be there in a minute," she says. "Don't go anywhere."

"Where am I going?"

Kaila raps the table. "Later, boss," she says.

I did have fun working with Kaila today. I thought it would bum me out and feel weird not going to Zoey's again, but what's really weird is how normal it feels. I still don't know if I'll ever get used to not spending Wednesdays at Zoey's, but I already know things will feel normal again, just differently normal.

Zoey wasn't in ELA yesterday or today. I don't know

why she wasn't, which is weird because before all this happened, I always knew where Zoey was. But not knowing where she's been these past couple of days has also felt differently normal.

"My turn," Mom says, dropping her coffee-stained dish towel on the table and sitting down across from me. "It's Mom and Silas time."

"What happened to your hand?" I ask.

She looks down. "What happened to it?"

"Your phone's not attached."

"You noticed," she says, smiling. "That makes me happy."

"Did you have it surgically removed?" I say. "I don't see any scars."

"I need to be more present, Silas," she says. "When I'm with you and your sisters, I need to be more present. I can't have my phone out all the time like I do. It's not healthy. I'm missing things, and I'm not one to miss things." She reaches across the table for my hand. "I'm trying, Silas."

"I know," I say.

"It may not look like I am, but I am. I'm always trying." She squeezes my fingers. "I know I have a lot going on, and Dad has a lot going on, but whatever we have going on is not more important than you."

"I know," I say again.

"It's important that you hear that." She lets go of my hand and sits up. "Dad and I have been talking, Silas. I think we've spoken more this past week than we have in . . . I don't know how long. And you know what? It's been good."

"Good," I say.

"It is good." She folds the dish towel. "We weren't talking about work or who was picking up or dropping off who. We were just talking."

"You hardly do anymore," I say.

"We do need to do a better job of communicating," she says. "One thing we did communicate is that we're both worried about you. And we feel helpless about it, and we don't want to feel helpless. We want—"

"I'm okay, Mom," I say.

She holds up her hand. "The other day, when you didn't want to go to practice—believe it or not—I was actually proud of you. I was. It's not selfish to look out for your own well-being. I was touched that you listened. Self-care should be a priority." She retucks her hair under her Jump & Grind cap. "I'm glad you didn't quit baseball, Silas. It would've made me sad because . . . do you know what I like best about the way you play?"

"That I play every play the same way," I say, nodding. "Like the game is always on the line. You tell me that all the time."

"I used to tell you that all the time," she says. "But I haven't recently. There are a lot of things I haven't been saying to you recently." She smiles. "Every time you're out there, Silas, you're playing like it could be the very last time you ever get to play. Baseball needs more players like that. The world needs more people like that—people who are passionate and energized. It's an indescribable feeling for a mother to see such passion and energy in her son. Don't ever lose that."

"You be you," I say softly.

"What's that?"

"Something Webb always tells me. You be you."

"Absolutely, Silas. Be authentic. It's the key to healthy relationships. Be authentic."

Authentic.

I think about Webb telling me to be authentic during our catch in center field. I think about Kaila telling me that she's authentic. I think about standing in the middle of Ms. Washington's class telling everyone about Glenn Burke, and how ever since—despite all that's happened— how I've never felt more authentic.

"You're not always going to feel like you fit in," Mom says. "No one does. But always be true to yourself, because if you are, people are going to rise up to you. Mark my words, Silas. The people in your life who choose to get to know you—who really get to know you—are going to be better off for it, so much better off. That's the type of person you are."

I stare across the table at Mom. She knows. I can't know for sure that she does, but she does. I think about all the videos where the kids talk about coming out to their moms, and when they asked them if they knew, they almost always said yes or they had a feeling or they were pretty sure. Mom knows or has a feeling or is pretty sure.

"Make note," she says, reaching into her pocket and holding up her phone. "This is the first time I've had it out."

"Noted," I say.

She checks the time. "We do need to get home to Dad and your sisters," she says. "But before we head out, I have to ask you one more thing."

"Yeah." My knees knock against the underside of the table.

She puts down the phone. "I need you to be honest."

I swallow.

"Is everything okay, Silas?" she asks.

"I think so."

"Are you sure?" She reaches across the table for my hand again.

"I think so . . . It's just . . . it's middle school, Mom. I'm trying to figure things out."

"That is what middle school is all about," she says. "And high school. And college. And life."

I'm trying not to cry, and Mom knows I'm trying not to cry because she knows what I look like when I'm trying not to cry.

"If everything wasn't okay," she says, "would you tell me?"

"Yes."

"Promise?"

"I promise."

She squeezes my hand. "I love you, Silas."

"I love you, too, Mom."

MY *SANDLOT*

"Bye, Dad," I say, opening the door before the car completely stops.

"I'll see you right here after practice, Silas," he says, leaning across the front seat as I get out.

"Thanks, Dad." I shut the door.

Jogging up the walkway to the field, I'm thinking I must be the first one here because I don't hear anyone on the other side of the bleachers. But practice starts at four forty-five, and it's already four thirty. By now, most the team is usually here, and—

I freeze on the warning track in foul territory and grab the top of my head. "No way!"

The Renegades *are* here.

"No way!" I say again. "You guys, this is nuts!"

The Renegades are lined up on the field dressed as *The Sandlot*. But they're not just dressed as *The Sandlot*. They're dressed and posing like the photo from the opening scene of the movie. Theo's all the way on the left, dressed like Benny, wearing a Dodgers cap, an open flannel shirt, and his baseball glove. Ben-Ben and Luis are in the middle. Ben-Ben's dressed as Smalls in blue jeans and a white shirt, and Luis is Squints, with his thick glasses, his black cap on backward, and his striped shirt. Luis's hand is on Kareem's shoulder. Kareem's dressed as Ham—white tee, white socks, jean shorts, and a catcher's mask on his head. His mitt is resting on the knob of his wooden bat. Jason's Yeah-Yeah, and Carter's Kenny DeNunez.

"This is nuts!" I'm still holding my head as I walk up. "You guys . . . how?"

No one answers. They just keep on posing. I look over at Webb by the backstop.

"This wasn't me," he says. "I had nothing to do with this."

"It was Zoey," Ben-Ben says.

"Zoey and her sister." Luis rubs the glasses on his shirt like Squints.

"And Malik," Ben-Ben says.

I let go of my head. "Malik?"

"He was at my house on Monday when Zoey came over."

"Zoey went to your house? How did Zoey—"

"Her sister brought her," Ben-Ben says. "She made her."

"Made her?"

"That's what she said." Ben-Ben holds up his hands. "Talk to Zoey."

"How'd you get all these outfits?" I ask. "And whose idea was it to pose like that?"

"All Malik," Luis says.

"You guys, this is nuts!"

"The Renegades are back!" Kareem says, holding up the catcher's mask.

"We are," I say, nodding. "We need to . . ." I look at my teammates. I breathe. "I think the Renegades need a handshake."

I wasn't planning this. The idea just popped into my

mind, and the words flew out of my mouth. But this time, I didn't want them back.

"What should it be?" Theo asks.

"A double high five," I say. I breathe again. "One for us and . . . and one for this guy, Glenn Burke. The guy who invented the high five."

"Invented?" Theo and Luis say together.

"Yeah," I say. "Glenn Burke gave the first-ever high five. I did a report on him in ELA. He played for the Los Angeles Dodgers in the 1970s and was their starting center fielder in the World Series one year."

"Was he any good?" Jason asks.

"He was great," I say, "but baseball never gave him the chance he deserved."

"Why haven't we ever heard of him?" Theo asks.

"That's . . . that's just how it is with some people," I say. "But it doesn't have to be."

"What say you, Renegades?" Webb says, walking over. "Are we talking today or practicing? Luis, why aren't we stretching yet?"

"You know what number he wore when he played for the Dodgers?" I point to Theo's jersey by his bag along the jouce. "Three."

"Savage!" Luis says.

"Benjamin Franklin 'the Jet' Rodriguez wore number three when he played for the Los Angeles Dodgers," I say, "and Glenn Burke wore number three when he played for the Los Angeles Dodgers."

"Pretty cool," Ben-Ben says.

"So our team handshake should be a double high five," I say. "We can have a high-five line before every game." I start swinging my arms and walking backward. "Two lines facing each other going toward home plate."

All my teammates—dressed like characters from *The Sandlot*—line up, and just like that, everything's like it used to be, but nothing's like it used to be because nothing will ever be like it used to be.

Me being me.

"Everyone goes down the line and double-high-fives everyone," I say. "Then, after the last person goes, we all meet at home plate. It's a high five for the Renegades and a high five for Glenn Burke."

38

ZOEY ALWAYS

I'm standing outside Zoey's front door tapping my Wiffle bat against the side of my head. I know I have to go inside, and I will go inside, but I'm still psyching myself.

Grace drove me here, and on our way up the driveway, I told her I needed a second before going in because it was still less than fifteen minutes ago that the bus had dropped me off at home from school and Grace had showed up—unannounced—to tell me she was taking me to see Zoey because what was going on between Zoey and me had gone on long enough.

The front door flies open.

"Are you coming in or not?" Grace says, and when I don't answer right away, she locks her arm in mine and pulls me in. "Someone's here to see you," she announces, dragging me into the kitchen.

"Hi, Silas," Dolores says. She's sitting at the kitchen table wearing her work clothes and checking a camera lens. "You're here to see me?"

"No, not you," Grace answers. "The moody one outside."

"Good." Dolores stands up and kisses my cheek. "I'm shooting a fiftieth anniversary party this evening, and I needed to be out the door five minutes ago."

"Have fun," I say.

Grace still has me by the arm, and with her free hand, she slides open the door to the back deck.

Zoey's sitting cross-legged and barefoot on one of the tan lounge chairs by the wooden planter boxes. She's got her orange-and-blue FC Cincinnati mini soccer ball in her lap and a large Ball jar of iced tea on the metal end table beside her.

"Sit," Grace says, unhooking my arm and pointing me to the other chaise lounge. "Talk."

She heads back in and shuts the sliding door. All of a sudden, Zoey and I are alone.

"What are you doing here?" she asks.

"What do you mean?" I say.

"I mean, what are you doing here?"

"Grace came to get me, and—"

"Grace drove you here?" she says, more statement than question. "Of course she did."

"I'm sorry, Zoey," I say. "I never should have said those things about you. I still can't believe I did."

Zoey looks at me but says nothing.

"I'd do anything to take it back," I say. "I really would. I hope—"

"What'd you bring that for?" She points to the bat across my knees. "In case things went bad?"

"Semaj," I say, holding it up. "She was in my room when Grace showed up. I saw the way she was looking at my bobbleheads, so I decided to take it with me. My bobbleheads are my bobbleheads."

Zoey double-dimple smiles, and I can't begin to explain how great it feels seeing her double-dimple smile. I knew I missed it, but I didn't realize how much I missed it until now.

"I really am sorry, Zoey," I say.

"I'm sorry, too," she says, tossing her soccer ball from hand to hand.

"What do you have to be sorry for?"

"I wasn't a good friend."

"You weren't a good friend? I was the one who lied about how you and I were—"

"No, Silas." She cuts me off. "I wasn't a good friend. When you first told me, I made it seem like . . . like I was okay with it and nothing had changed, but that wasn't . . . that wasn't true."

"Zoey, you don't need to—"

"It did change things," she says. "For me, it did. But it shouldn't, and I know it shouldn't, and it won't, but when you told me, it did. And it has. Is this making any sense?"

I shrug. "Maybe?"

"It's different when it's real, Silas. I know how I'm supposed to react because it's not supposed to make a difference, and it doesn't. It really doesn't. But it does. When you first find out, it does make a difference. When it involves you, it's . . . it's confusing. I know it shouldn't be, and I don't want it to be, and . . ." She covers her mouth. "Grace told me I was being a horrible friend, and she was right."

"Grace?"

"I didn't tell her. I kept my promise."

"But she knows?"

"Remember how I told you she once asked me if you were gay?"

I smile. "Yeah, I think I remember you saying something about that."

"I thought you would." She double-dimples again. "Well, on Sunday, after the last *Bye Bye Birdie*, we were hanging out—and we hadn't hung out in the longest time because of the show and all—and she started asking what was up between us. So we started talking, and then I asked her if she remembered a while back asking me . . ." Zoey stops and touches my knee. "I swear, that's as far as I got. I never finished the sentence. She guessed it."

I flip my hair. "That sounds like Grace," I say.

"She went off on me, Silas," Zoey says. "Like, seriously went off on me. Even after I told her what you did." She stands up and starts juggling the soccer ball with her bare feet. "Don't get me wrong, she thought what you did was awful, but she said what I did was even worse. You're going through like the hardest thing you've ever done . . . and you chose to tell me. You came out to *me*, Silas. You told *me* you were gay, and then a few days later, I'm telling you I hated you and never wanted to speak to you again."

"But only because I—"

"It doesn't matter," Zoey says. "I'm your best friend, Silas. What kind of friend does that? I wasn't there for you when you needed me. Best friends don't do that. No matter what."

"Did you ever almost tell anyone about me?"

"Never."

"Not even Ben-Ben?" I reach for her tea.

"Never." She catches the ball. "I would never do that to you. I would never do that to anyone."

I take a sip and put it back down. "I still can't believe I never realized you and Ben-Ben were in the same robotics club."

I pick up the bat and motion for her to pitch the ball. She underhands it to me, but the ball is heavier than the bat, and even though I swing hard, the ball goes straight down.

"Nice hit." Zoey traps the ball with her heel, flips it up, and starts juggling again. "Do you know how Grace found out we had a fight?"

"How?"

"Ms. Washington told her about the argument we had in class."

The ball hits off the side of her knee and bounces toward the steps at the end of the deck. I pop off my chair and grab it before it rolls onto the lawn.

"I went to see Ben-Ben after school on Monday," Zoey says, sitting down on the top step.

"You waved at me when you walked into class on Monday." I sit down beside her.

"Almost waved."

We both laugh, and I can't begin to explain how great it feels to laugh with Zoey again, because I knew I missed laughing with her, but I didn't realize how much I missed laughing with her until now.

"Grace took me to Ben-Ben's," Zoey says.

"How'd you know where he lives?"

"We sometimes drive him home from robotics," she says.

"He never missed a practice or game," I say. "He got to a few practices late, but everyone does. Maybe that's why I never realized you were in the same robotics club." I shrug. "Who knows?"

"I didn't know Malik would be there," she says. "I didn't even know they were friends."

"Ben-Ben told me Malik was there."

She bumps my shoulder. "You never told me how cute he was."

I give her a look.

"Well, he is cute, right?" She double-dimples and bumps me again. "Kinda sorta?"

"Kinda sorta," I say, softly.

I smile weirdly because everything about Zoey's saying that to me feels weird, even though it shouldn't feel weird.

"Malik came up with the *Sandlot* idea," she says. "He knew that Grace let you borrow the outfits. He asked if we still had them, and when I said yes, he came up with the idea."

"That sounds like Malik," I say. I breathe. "It's all happening so fast, Zoey. My whole life is different now. All of a sudden, everything is different. And it gets more different every day." I look at her. "But then at the same time, nothing's changed."

"You sound very drama queen right now," she says, double-dimpling. "I can say that now, you know."

I smile weirdly again. "I guess."

"Yes, I can say that now. That was very drama queen." She touches my arm. "Just so you know, I knew you were gay before you told me."

"*What?*"

She's still double-dimpling. "I did."

"Zoey. I'm not ready to joke about—"

"You fart rainbows," she says.

I laugh. I can't help it.

"It's true," she says. "Everyone knows gay kids fart rainbows. Multicolored farts are the universal sign of queer kids."

I stare. She said the word *queer*. She knows I noticed.

"Jack Will," I say.

"What?"

I pick up the mini soccer ball from the step between us and trace my finger along the blue border of the FC Cincinnati logo.

"Promise not to laugh?" I say without looking up.

"No way," she says. "I'm not promising that."

I half smile. "Jack Will," I say again. "That's how I knew for sure."

"What do you mean?"

"Last year, they always showed the movie *Wonder* during indoor recess. And every time we watched it . . . every time we watched it . . ."

"Yeah?"

I look up. "Every time we watched it, I wanted to hold Jack Will's hand." I breathe. "When we were sitting at your kitchen table the other day, you asked me when I knew. That's when . . . that's when I knew for sure."

Zoey double-dimple grins. "That's awesome."

"Thanks," I say.

"Jack Will was pretty cute in that movie." She takes the soccer ball from me. "Not as cute as Malik, but he was pretty cute."

It's so weird hearing her say that about Malik to me, but at the same time, it's not weird at all.

"The Renegades have a new team handshake," I say. "A double high five." I hold up my hands.

She puts the soccer ball between her knees and smacks them both.

"One for the Renegades," I say, "and one for Glenn Burke."

"They know about Glenn Burke?"

"I told them," I say.

"Seriously?"

"That he invented the high five. Not that he was gay and—"

"Good for you, Silas," she says. She squeezes the ball with the heels of her hands. "I mean it. That's awesome you told them."

"Before the start of every game," I say, "we're going to have a high-five line, and . . . and every time we do it, I'm going to take a second to think about Glenn Burke because . . . because my high five for Glenn Burke isn't only because he invented the high five. My high five . . . he was first. Glenn Burke deserves a high five."

"Awesome, Silas."

I reach into my pocket and pull out a couple of the high-five stickers.

"Here," I say, handing them to her. "Haley made these."

"Wow, she drew these? She's getting so good."

"Really good," I say.

"You told her about Glenn Burke?"

"Only about the high five."

Zoey peels one off its paper and sticks it to the soccer ball.

"I found a bunch of them stuck to my bulletin board the other day," I say. "She has no idea how much it meant to me seeing them."

"Haley's pretty awesome."

"Sometimes," I say. I rub my eyes with both palms. "I'm going to tell my mom."

"You are? Silas, that's—"

"Not now and maybe not . . . I will tell her. She'll be next."

"I think you should," Zoey says. "Erica is so cool."

"You don't have to live with her."

"You know she's cool, Silas." She bops me on the head with the ball.

I duck away. "I guess."

"No, she is. Erica is so cool, and you know it. Say it."

"I'm not saying it."

She bops me harder. "Say it!"

I block the ball. "My mom is cool! My mom is cool!" I stand up. "Happy now?"

"Now, that wasn't so difficult, was it?" She gets up and plants the ball in my chest.

"Can I ask you . . . can I ask you for a favor?" I place

my hands over hers. "Will you help me . . . will you help me with my coming-out video?"

"Yes!" She throws the ball into the air. "I'd love to!"

"I'm not posting it on YouTube or anything," I say. "I just want to make one. For the future me to watch someday."

"That's awesome, Silas."

"But I don't want to make it yet. I just—"

"Whatever you want, Silas." She puts her hands on my shoulders. "You decide."

"And let me be the one to ask you about it, okay? Like, don't ask me about it. When I'm ready to make it, you'll be the first to know." I squeeze her fingers. "I promise."

"I'll help you under one condition."

"Uh-oh," I say.

"Uh-oh is right," she says. "We need to sing. I *need* me some karaoke."

"What do you want to sing?" I ask.

She double-dimple grins.

"Why are you smiling like that? Is this the uh-oh part?"

She takes my hand and starts dancing toward the door.

"Are these like the gayest songs you can think of?" I ask.

She squeezes my hand and lifts our arms. "You know it!"

39

A HIGH FIVE FOR GLENN BURKE

"Renegades are what?" I shout.

"Renegades are ready!" my teammates shout back.

We're all on the field before the start of our double-header against the Warriors. We're in front of our dugout in two lines facing one another—our high-five line. I'm at the end closest to home plate, standing in the middle. Webb and Coach Rockford are at the other end, facing each other.

I cup my hand around my ear. "Renegades are what?" I yell louder.

"Renegades are ready!" they yell back even louder.

I point to our bleachers behind the dugout. "Renegades are what?"

"Renegades are ready!" everyone shouts.

And when I say everyone, I do mean everyone, especially for me. Mom and Dad are both here. Semaj is sitting between them. Haley's in front of them next to Zoey, who's wearing the Dodgers cap and the number three Dodgers jersey. Grace is on the other side of Zoey, and Ms. Washington's on the other side of Grace. It's so awesome seeing Grace and Ms. Washington here because neither of them have ever been to one of my games. And it's awesome seeing Kaila sitting on the other side of Mom.

"Here we go, Renegades!" I point down the line with both index fingers and slide next to Ben-Ben.

Webb starts double-high-fiving the Renegades on his line, and Coach Rockford starts double-high-fiving the Renegades on his. When they reach the end, they cross over and double-high-five all the Renegades on the other line until they're back to where they started but on the opposite sides. Then they run down the middle, and when they get to the end, they double-high-five each other and step back into the lines.

Ernesto and Alexander go next and do the same thing. Then Jason and Carter go, and then the others, and then suddenly, because we have an odd number of players now, I'm the only one who hasn't double-high-fived my teammates.

I start with Ben-Ben, who's next to me, but instead of double-high-fiving Luis, who's next to him, I jump across to Kareem, the last person on the other side. Then I jump back across to Luis and double-high-five him, and I do this all the way down the line until I reach Webb. And when we double-high-five, for a moment, we lock our fingers.

"You be you," he says.

"Me be me," I say back.

I sprint for home plate and jump on it with both feet, and when I do, I take a second like I said I would. I think about Glenn Burke. I think about him standing at home plate and giving Dusty Baker that very first high five. I think about what could have been and should have been for Glenn Burke. I think about all the opportunities he never got to have and all the opportunities I will. I think about how I wouldn't be standing here right now if it wasn't for Glenn Burke.

"Let's do this, Renegades!" I shout and wave to my teammates. "Let's do this."

ACKNOWLEDGMENTS

A High Five for Glenn Burke would not exist without the help and support of so many, and if I was to come anywhere close to properly thanking everyone, these acknowledgments would far exceed the length of this book.

With that said, eternal gratitude, love, and light to ...

Erin Murphy, my agent. Thank you for your encouragement, support, and friendship. Thank you for knowing I had this book in me. Thank you for pushing me to tell this story, part of my truth.

Wes Adams, my editor. Thank you for your unparalleled vision, guidance, and wisdom. You saw a middle grade novel on the pages of a picture-book manuscript and patiently worked with me as I *Frindle*-d the text.

Farrar Straus Giroux and the entire Macmillan Children's Publishing Group. Thank you especially to Melissa Warten, Avia Perez, Ana Deboo, Cassie Gonzales, Celeste Cass, Mary Van Akin, Kelsey Marrujo, Katie Halata, Lucy Del Priore, and Joy Peskin.

Aaron Katzman, Julie Lenk, Sandy London, Anna Rekate, and Audrey Vernick. Thank you for reading early versions of the manuscript and for providing the expert insights and feedback I craved. Aaron, I kept score, too; Sandy, I *peeped* too much; and Julie, I will never bring a cowbell to a baseball game.

John Cook, Cole Lenk, and Jackson Parrish. Thank you to my baseball all-star team. Thanks for telling me all about your batter's box routines, your coaches, your dugout chants, your hygiene (ew!), and your love for the game.

Kameron Wright and Leo Puvilland. Thanks for helping me understand robotics just enough so that I was able to pretend to know what I was talking about.

Laurie Halse Anderson. Thanks for joining me on that bitter-cold, early-morning walk around Washington, DC, a few Decembers ago. It was a circle-the-calendar moment. I felt it then; I know it now. You can't fix broken people.

Kari Anne Holt. Thanks for walking the talk, and for giving me the courage to speak my truth more forcefully, and for enabling me to speak more knowledgeably about the ghosting of books. Our very existence is not controversial.

Matt Bomer and Jose Llana. Thanks for setting the example. You were the role models I needed when I was a kid. Thanks for being that role model to so many kids today.

Corey Anker, Steven Gershowitz, Eddie Liao, and Wendy Lieber. Thanks for being there when I came out, for being there when I needed it most. Steven, thanks for being the definition of a friend since we were eleven. I wouldn't be here without you.

The Big Apple Softball League. Thanks for introducing me to Ernesto Reyes. Our New York City team that finished in third place in the 2001 Gay World Series was legendary.

Billy Bean, Jason Collins, Wade Davis, Greg Louganis, Martina Navratilova, Megan Rapinoe, Robbie Rogers, Sheryl Swoopes, and all the other out gay athletes who paved the way and showed the world that everyone can play.

ESPN *30 for 30* documentary series. Thank you for introducing Glenn Burke to so many.

Doug Harris, the coproducer of *Out: The Glenn Burke Story*, the documentary film about Glenn Burke. Thanks for taking the time to speak with me and share your stories.

Cheryl, my sister, and Alex and Ethan, my nephews. You all rock . . . And perhaps since I acknowledged you, you'll even read the book!

Debbie and Bill, my parents. For never wavering, for never flinching—not once—after July 24, 1996.

Katniss, our beautiful rescue dog, who brings such joy to everyone and provides me with ample playtime breaks.

Kevin, my husband. *My husband.* Words a previous, self-hating version of me would've never been able to process, comprehend, or accept. Words I now say loud and proud. I love you.